Joseph Allen

Life of Nelson

Joseph Allen

Life of Nelson

ISBN/EAN: 9783337415112

Printed in Europe, USA, Canada, Australia, Japan

Cover: Foto ©Raphael Reischuk / pixelio.de

More available books at **www.hansebooks.com**

ROUTLEDGE'S WORLD LIBRARY

"Syllables govern the World."—JOHN SELDEN.

LIFE OF NELSON

BY

JOSEPH ALLEN

WITH AN INTRODUCTION

BY THE

REV. HUGH REGINALD HAWEIS, M.A.

"All agree there is but one Nelson"
—EARL ST. VINCENT

LONDON

GEORGE ROUTLEDGE AND SONS

BROADWAY, LUDGATE HILL

NEW YORK: 9 LAFAYETTE PLACE

1886

INTRODUCTION TO LIFE OF NELSON.

NELSON was probably the greatest fighting captain that ever sailed the seas. Better navigators there may have been—indeed, Nelson's own officers more than once demurred, and with some reason, to his lordship's habit of interfering with the ship; but in an age of distinguished Admirals the ablest of them was proud to yield the palm to one whose insight, daring, and infinite resource in battle paralysed the navies of the world, and left no gun upon all the wide seas to reply to the last broadside at Trafalgar.

Nelson, Napoleon, Washington, and Wellington were all contemporaries. Nelson was eleven years older than Wellington and Napoleon (who were both born in the same year, 1769), and twenty-six years younger than Washington.

Of these four mighty captains, Napoleon was alone a ruthless destroyer. The other three were constructive, conservative, or both.

Washington was the creator of a nation and the saviour of a continent which England had proved herself unfit to hold any longer.

Napoleon was simply the bloody scourge of Europe—immolating as many nations as he could get at to one idol—himself.

Nelson broke Napoleon's power by sea at Trafalgar in 1803, and Wellington finished him on shore at Waterloo in 1815.

To extraordinary professional gifts, Nelson united a personality altogether magnetic and irresistible. The most mutinous crew became suddenly loyal as soon as he came on board. The jealousies of rival admirals were laid aside, and the cavils of cabinets silenced. On more than one

occasion common sailors rushed between their beloved captain and his foe, and received the sabre stroke or the bullet
intended for him.

He carried his frail—and, as time went on—maimed body
(he had lost an arm and an eye) with such dignity that kings
rose instinctively, like suppliants, on his approach. His
simple faith and generosity won all hearts, and even his
enemies confessed that his iron bravery was tempered with
the noblest humanity.

The French prisoners were awed at the solemn religious
services that he caused to be held on board the *Vanguard*
immediately after the battle of the Nile, and observed that
English officers who could in the midst of such confusion
and excitement so inspire their men with religion, must
necessarily prove victorious.

In my enforced curtailment of Mr. Joseph Allen's able
biography I have been obliged to omit many interesting
details, and have refrained from entering into the delicate
question of Nelson's separation from his wife, and his relations with Lady Hamilton, but a reference to the following
books will enable the student to fill up the inevitable gaps
should he feel, and I hope he may, inspired to take that
trouble :

JAMES HARRISON. "The Life of Lord Nelson." 2 vols. (An early
but inflated narrative.)
SOUTHEY's "Life of Nelson." I vol. (A standard popular book.)
CLARKE AND MCARTHUR. "Life and Services of Horatio Viscount
Nelson " 3 vols. (A popular compilation spun out.)
SIR HARRY NICOLAS. "Nelson's Life and Letters," 7 vols. (Ex-
haustive on Nelson's personality.)
PETTIGREW's "Life of Nelson." (Gossiping, but most useful and
full of detail).
JOSEPH ALLEN's "Life of Nelson." (Brief, but derived from personal
and reliable sources) CHARNOCK AND WHITE may also be con-
sulted.

CONTENTS

LIFE OF LORD NELSON

—◈—

ON Michaelmas day, 1758, in the unpretending parsonage-house of Burnham Thorpe, near Wells, Nelson first beheld the light. His father, the Rev. Edmund Nelson, had held the rectory of Burnham nearly fifty years. The maiden name of his mother was Suckling: her grandmother was an elder sister of Sir Robert Walpole, and Horatio was named after his god-father, the first Lord Walpole. Horatio was the sixth child.

Nine years after the birth of our hero, his mother died, leaving eight children. Captain Maurice Suckling, the maternal uncle of our hero, on the death of Mrs. Nelson, offered to take one of the boys under his care, and Horatio became his uncle's *protégé*. He was forthwith sent to the High School at Norwich, from which he was removed to a School at North Walsham. On one occasion, during the winter holidays, Horatio and his brother William set off on horseback to return to school; but there having been a fall of snow, William, the elder brother, thinking the snow too deep, and, perhaps, not very desirous to leave home, refused to proceed. On the return of the boys, their father did not insist upon their venturing at all hazards, but desired them to make another attempt, adding, "I shall leave it to your honour." Although the snow was sufficiently deep, and the road bad enough to have warranted their turning back a second time, Horatio persisted in advancing. The words "I will leave it to your honour," rang in his ears, and no inducement on the part of his brother could shake his resolution. On another occasion, the embryo hero is reported to have robbed his schoolmaster's pear tree, because no one else was bold enough to attempt it.

His educational course, however, was cut short by an unexpected event. In 1770, a conflict with Spain threatened, and Captain Suckling, being one of the most distinguished officers of his standing in the Navy, was appointed to command the 64-gun ship *Raisonable*, fitting for commission at Chatham. Burning with irrepressible ardour for naval glory, or possibly anxious, like other boys, to be freed from scholastic trammels, Horatio petitioned his father to allow him to go to join his uncle. With the blunt good nature which characterizes the profession of a sailor, Captain Suckling wrote in reply to his brother-in-law's request to be allowed to send the boy to his ship,—"What has poor Horatio done, who is so weak, that he above all the rest should be sent to rough it at sea? But let him come," he added, "and the first time that we go into action, a cannon-ball may knock off his head, and provide for him at once."

Every biographer of Nelson has recorded the anecdote that when a mere child he was scolded by his grandmother, for absenting himself an unusual time from his home. "I wonder, child," said the old lady, "that hunger and fear did not drive you home." "Fear," he replied,—"I never saw fear,—what is it?"

The emulative spirit and restless desire to be in action was not long without receiving legitimate occupation. An Arctic expedition was projected. The attempt to solve the problem, and effect the north-west passage, which has so long foiled the most vigorous and scientific efforts of enterprising men, was then about to be made under the direction of Captains Constantine John Phipps and Skeffington Lutwidge. The ships engaged were the *Racehorse* and *Carcass*, and although no boys were allowed to enter for the service, young Nelson managed to get appointed to the latter ship. The expedition excited considerable interest, and the ships prior to their departure were personally inspected by Lord Sandwich, then first lord of the Admiralty. The *Racehorse* and *Carcass* sailed from the Nore on the 4th June, 1773. On the 28th they made Spitzbergen, where they were beset, and by the end of July, when in nearly 80° of latitude, longitude 18° 48′ east, their further progress was arrested by impenetrable fields and barriers of ice. The difficulty was to return and avoid the alternative of passing the winter

" In thrilling regions of thick-ribbed ice."

Exertions were, therefore, employed to cut the ships out, and, considering the great difficulty which must have been experienced from the want of proper ice-implements, their escape from being blocked must have been chiefly due to the co-operation of nature. The currents which have been known to set ships many hundreds of miles doubtless contributed to render the efforts of the men successful. Their labours were unremitting ; but the ice in many parts was twelve feet thick. Preparations were made to abandon the ships. Nelson was placed in charge of one of the cutters, and all was got ready, in case the ships should continue fixed in the ice. They were unprepared for wintering, and their only chance of preservation rested in the doubtful resource of dragging the boats to the edge of the ice, and so escaping to some whaling-ships in the vicinity. The wind, however, came from the N.N.E., and all sail being set, the ships gradually forced their way through the ice, and on the 10th August reached Smeerenberg Harbour.

While the ships were in the ice, during the middle watch, Nelson stole unperceived from his ship, and set out with a young companion in pursuit of a bear. A fog arose, which for several hours hid the adventurers from their anxious companions on ship-board. With the early dawn, however, they were espied in close action with a huge bear, and depending on the butt ends of their muskets, as their ammunition had been expended. The signal to return was made, but apparently disregarded, and it was not until Captain Lutwidge fired a gun that the bear was driven from his combat, and the midshipmen hastened back, not a little alarmed for the probable conse-quences of their trespass. To his captain's reprimand Nelson had but one reply,—" I wished, sir, to kill the bear, that I might carry the skin to my father."

The ships remained a short time on the coast of Greenland, but finding
no chance of re-entering the ice or of prosecuting the object of the expedition,
they returned to England and were paid off. The varied service our hero
had hitherto undergone had had a most beneficial effect upon his constitution. The sickliness had apparently been succeeded by robust health ; and
possibly, had he remained in a temperate climate a few years, his body would
have become healthy and strong, as his mind was vigorous. But it is a
necessary part of a sailor's duty to go wherever the service leads him ; and
from the Arctic regions Nelson proceeded to the East Indies. The 20-gun
frigate *Seahorse*, commanded by Captain Richard Farmar, who afterwards
distinguished himself by his heroic defence and self-immolation when commanding the *Quebec* in action with the French frigate *Surveillante*, was
destined to bear our hero from the frigid to the torrid zone.

A voyage to India was then an affair of five or six months ; and from the
defective victualling of the navy, it was no unusual thing for a ship to arrive
at her destination with half the crew in the sick-list from scurvy or fever.
The climate of the East Indies proved most injurious to Nelson, and in less
than eighteen months he was compelled to invalid. His limbs began to lose
their powers, and permanent lameness appeared his fate. He was accordingly
sent on board the *Dolphin*. The change saved his life, and restored him to
active exertions, but the disease was too deeply seated to be quickly eradi-
cated. The feeling of his difficulties weighed heavily on his mind, and he
began to despair of ultimate success. "After a gloomy reverie," as he afterwards expressed himself, "a sudden glow of patriotism was kindled within
me, and presented my king and country as my patron. Well then, I exclaimed,
I will be a hero, and, confiding in Providence, I will brave every danger."

Doubtless there are periods in the lives of most great men when the future
seems to be darkly revealed. It is impossible in any other way to reconcile
Nelson's early visions of future eminence with his then humble position. It
was a time of peace. His health had received a severe shock. He had
neither money nor, as he thought, friends to assist him through the world ;
but, in despite of all these obstacles, as he often said years afterwards to his
friend Captain Hardy, a radiant orb seemed displayed before him, which
urged him onward to renown. But during his absence from England, his
patron, Captain Suckling, had obtained the post of comptroller of the Navy

Board, and our hero's prospects were not so hopeless as he thought they were. On being paid off from the *Dolphin*, he was appointed acting-lieutenant of the 64-gun ship *Worcester*, Captain Mark Robinson. In this ship he proceeded with a convoy to Gibraltar, and on his return, having served the requisite length of time, he passed his examination for a lieutenant. The following characteristic letter, dated April 14, 1777, written at the Navy-office, and addressed to his brother William, refers to this important era in a naval officer's life.

"I passed my degree as master of arts on the 9th instant (that is, passed the lieutenant's examination), and received my commission on the following day for a fine frigate of thirty-two guns. So I am now left in the world to shift for myself, which I hope I shall do, so as to bring credit to myself and friends. I am sorry there is no possibility this time of seeing each other, but I hope the time will come in a few years when we will spend some merry hours together. [N.B. If it is not too troublesome, turn over.] Where we shall go at present, I know not ; but wherever it is, I will always write to you. If you ever choose to write, inclose either to Mr. Suckling or my brother, as in all probability they will know where we are gone. I leave London on Wednesday evening, so shall always be glad to hear from you. Believing me to be, dear brother, your affectionate brother,

"HORATIO NELSON."

"P.S. Pray give my best respects to my old schoolfellow, H. Hammond."

The passing certificate states :—"He produceth journals kept by himself in the *Carcass*, *Seahorse*, *Dolphin*, and *Worcester*, and certificates from Captains Suckling, Lutwidge, Farmar, Pigott, and Robinson, of his diligence, &c. He can splice, knot, reef a sail, &c., and is qualified to do the duty of an able seaman and midshipman." Dated the 9th of April, 1777, and signed M. S., John Campbell, and Abraham North, captains. M. S. were the initials of Captain Maurice Suckling, Nelson's uncle, the comptroller of the navy, who was present at the examination by virtue of his office. Nelson's biographers relate the following interesting anec-dote. "At the head of the table sat his uncle Maurice, as comptroller of the navy, who had purposely concealed his relationship from the examining captain. When his nephew had recovered from his confusion, his answers

were prompt and satisfactory, and indicated the talents he so eminently
possessed. The examination ended in a manner very honourable to him,
upon which his uncle immediately threw off his reserve, and rising from his
seat, introduced his nephew. The examining captains expressed their
surprise at his not having informed them of this before. 'No,' replied the
independent comptroller, 'I did not wish the younker to be favoured ; I
felt convinced that he would pass a good examination, and you see, gentlemen, I have not been disappointed.' "

No sooner had our hero passed this ordeal than an appointment awaited
him to the 32-gun frigate *Lowestoffe*. Here he had the good fortune to
be placed under a very intelligent, experienced, and kind-hearted commander, Captain William Locker, who was destined to nourish the seeds
of greatness inherent in his lieutenant, not only commanded his respect,
but laid the foundation of a friendship which terminated only with death.
The *Lowestoffe* was sent to the Jamaica station, to protect the British
trade from the depredations of French and American privateers, and
Nelson was frequently employed in the *Lowestoffe's* tenders, in which he
made several captures. It was here that he gained particular notice by
volunteering, in a gale of wind, to board an American letter of marque,
which had been nearly swamped by carrying a heavy press of sail. The
master of the *Lowestoffe* also volunteered, but was told that it would be
his turn next.

While serving in the *Lowestoffe*, Nelson had the misfortune to lose his
kind patron, Captain Suckling ; but he had already established for himself
a good reputation as a seaman and officer ; and Sir Peter Parker, who commanded on the station, generously supplied the lost place of his uncle. Sir
Peter took our hero into the 50-gun ship *Bristol*, and on the 8th of December,
1778, appointed him master and commander of the *Badger* brig. In this
vessel he rendered considerable service to the merchants, by the protection
of the trade from the privateers.

While the *Badger* was lying in Montego Bay, Jamaica, the *Glasgow*
frigate, Captain Thomas Lloyd, anchored in the bay, and two hours afterwards was discovered to be on fire. The boats of the different ships in the
bay were quickly alongside, and those of the *Badger*, in command of Nelson.
He boarded the *Glasgow*, and assisted Captain Lloyd in his endeavours to

preserve order, and to save the lives of the crew. The magazine was cleared under his superintendence, and the beds and quoins removed from under the guns, which, by elevating their muzzles, prevented damage to the ships in the bay, as the guns were discharged by the heat.

Promotion kept pace with our hero's merits, and on the 11th of June, 1779, being then in his twenty-first year, he was made a post captain, and appointed to command the 28-gun frigate *Hinchinbrook*. The *Hinchinbrook* was a wretched tub—an old merchant ship sheathed with wood, and about the last description of ship to suit a man like Nelson. D'Estaing having threatened Jamaica, Nelson tendered his services to Governor-General Dalling, and was appointed to command the batteries of Fort Charles and Port Royal.

But D'Estaing abandoned the project, and General Dalling was free to attempt the execution of a design he had formed against Fort Juan, situated on the River Juan, leading to Lake Nicaragua. The plan, which embraced the acquisition of a small empire, was well conceived ; but unforeseen delays and important omissions occurred in the equipment of the expedition. These causes were fatal. The delay exposed those engaged in the expedition to the deadly effects of the sickliest season. The *Hinchinbrook* was selected for this service, and Nelson appointed to command the naval portion. On the 24th of March, 1780, the expedition, consisting of 500 men, regulars and volunteers, under Major Polson, entered the San Juan. Here Nelson's instructions ended ; but so blind had been the projectors, that no pilots for the river had been provided, and no one appeared to know anything of the navigation or position of the fort to be attacked. It was not Nelson s nature to desert his countrymen in their difficulties, nor to turn back while anything remained· to be done or attempted. It was the dry season ; the river was low, and impeded with banks and shallows ; the Indian allies were nearly useless, and the soldiers could hardly contend with the heat. On Nelson and his sailors, therefore, devolved the labour and danger of the toilsome passage. At length the small out-fort of San Bartholomew was reached, where, on an island, a semicircular battery of ten small swivels commanded the approaches. At the head of a few seamen, Nelson leaped on shore, left his shoes on the muddy bank, and, barefooted, "boarded the battery." San Juan was still sixteen miles distant, and two days more hard labour elapsed before its fortifications were reached. Nelson advised an immediate attack, but his counsel, unhappily, was not followed, and the slow formalities of a siege commenced in a low, marshy place, under a scorching sun.

The neighbouring woods were infested with all sorts of venomous reptiles. One of the men was bitten by a snake, and in a few hours his body was putrid. Nelson, who slept in a hammock suspended to the bough of a tree, nearly shared the same fate. A snake was found coiled away at the foot of his hammock, and he escaped only through the watchfulness of the Indians. He experienced another escape from death, having drunk from a fountain poisoned by the boughs of manchineel. Fort San Juan surrendered on the 24th April, but the gain was little other than a severe loss. Previously to this, the besiegers were so much in want of provisions, that they lived upon monkey broth. A pestilence ravaged the conquerors as well as the conquered ; and the castle, after a few months, reverted to its original possessors —disease and death having done infinitely more than Spanish bullets. Out of 1,800 men despatched on this service, not more than 380 returned. The *Hinchinbrook's* crew comprised 200 men, of whom eighty-seven fell sick in one night, and very few, — not more than ten, — survived this service. Fortunately for the subject of our memoir, he was withdrawn before it was too late. A vacancy occurred in the command of the 44-gun ship *Janus*, which Sir Peter Parker,bestowed upon him.

It is a singular coincidence, that up to this period, and, in fact, through-out the whole of his career, Nelson was followed by his friend Collingwood. On Nelson leaving the *Lowestoffe*, Collingwood was appointed to that ship, and the same with reference to his joining the *Bristol*, and promotion into the *Badger*, and *Hinchinbrook*. In the last scene of Nelson's eventful life also, Collingwood was still his friend and successor. The removal of Nelson from the pestilential region of San Juan, saved him from sharing the fate which attended most of his companions. He had been attacked with dysentery, and was recalled barely in time to save his life. He reached Jamaica more dead than alive the day prior to the surrender of San Juan. He was conveyed on shore in his cot, and although he had recovered in some degree the use of his limbs, he found himself quite unable to continue in command of the *Janus*. He therefore invalided, and took passage in the

Lion, commanded by the Honourable William Cornwallis, who treated him with that humane attention which was never forgotten. On his return to England, Nelson, according to the fashion of the day, resorted to Bath. He was so helpless that he was obliged to be lifted in and out of his bed, and it took three months before he recovered the use of his limbs.

But no sooner had he acquired strength enough to move about, than he was to be seen again an eager candidate for employment. The war was still proceeding, and his request was not denied. On the 16th August, 1781, he was appointed to command the 28-gun frigate *Albemarle*, at Woolwich. This ship had been a short time previously captured from the French, and purchased into the service. The fatigue attendant upon equipping the ship for sea was almost too much for Nelson's enfeebled frame. Writing to his friend Captain Locker he said, " I have been so ill as hardly to be kept out of bed, and have been but twice out of the ship." The *Albemarle* was ordered to proceed to Elsineur, to protect the homeward-bound trade from the Baltic ; and the *Argo* and *Enterprise* were also placed under Nelson's orders for this purpose. It was the period of armed neutrality when the squadron anchored off Elsineur. A Danish midshipman was despatched by the admiral to take down the particulars of the ships. " This," said Nelson, to the young officer, on his boarding the *Albemarle*, " is one of His Britannic Majesty's ships ; you are at liberty to count the guns as you go down the side, and you may assure your admiral that if necessary they shall be well served." The asperities, however, soon wore off, salutes were exchanged, and reciprocal civilities ensued. The service was safely performed under the orders of Captain Dickson in the *Sampson*, he being the senior officer, and the *Albemarle* arrived in the Downs on the 3rd of January, 1782.

On the 20th of October, the *Albemarle* sailed with a convoy for New York. Admiral Digby, the commander-in-chief on the station, a friend of Nelson's late uncle, Captain Suckling, congratulated our hero on coming upon a station where prize-money was to be made. " Yes, sir,' replied Nelson ; "but the West Indies is the station for honour." And at the instigation of Lord Hood, who was then at Sandy Hook, the *Albemarle* was ordered to accompany his division of the fleet to the West Indies. Nelson was not long before he obtained the entire confidence of Lord Hood, who was, perhaps, the first officer of his rank in the service. It was on this station that Nelson first became acquainted with Prince William Henry—our late sailor king, William IV. In a letter to Captain Locker he thus mentions his position, and gives an opinion respecting the young prince :—

" My situation in Lord Hood's fleet must be in the highest degree flattering to a young man. He [Lord Hood] treats me as if I was his son, and will, I am convinced, give me anything I can ask of him ; nor is my situation with Prince William less flattering. Lord Hood was so kind as to tell him (indeed, I cannot make use of expressions strong enough to describe what I felt) that if he wished to ask questions relative to ' Naval Tactics,' I could give him as much information as any officer in the fleet. He will be, I am certain, an ornament to our service. He is a seaman which you could hardly suppose ; every other qualification you may expect of him. But he will be a disciplinarian, and a strong one : he says he is determined every person shall serve his time before they shall be provided for, as he is obliged to serve his. A vast deal of notice has been taken of him at Jamaica ; with the best temper and great good sense, he cannot fail of being pleasing to every one."

Nelson's personal appearance at this time is described as very singular. The Duke of Clarence, subsequently speaking of him, said, " I was then a midshipman on board the *Barfleur*, when Captain Nelson came alongside in his barge, who appeared the merest boy of a captain I ever beheld. He had on a full-laced uniform, his lank unpowdered hair was tied in a stiff Hessian tail of an extraordinary length, and the old-fashioned flaps of his waistcoat, added to the general quaintness of his figure, particularly attracted my notice. There was something irresistibly pleasing in his address and conversation ; and an enthusiasm when speaking on professional subjects that showed he was no common being."

The *Albemarle* was ordered to cruise off La Guayra, but beyond the fact of Nelson's detaining a Spanish launch, and hospitably entertaining the officers and crew (including a German prince), who had been engaged in botanical pursuits, no incident is recorded worthy of notice. News of peace having arrived, the *Albemarle* was ordered home. The ship arrived at Spithead 25th June, 1783, and was paid off at Portsmouth on the 3rd July.

So popular was Nelson, that, although at the time seamen were very much disgusted at their treatment in the service, the whole ship's company volunteered to go with him if he could obtain command of another ship. On reaching London, Lord Hood presented Captain Nelson at court, where he was very graciously received by the king. Writing to his friend Mr. Hercules Ross, he makes use of the following magnanimous remarks :— "True honour, I hope, predominates in my mind far above riches. I have closed the war without a fortune ; but I trust and, from the attention that has been paid to me, believe, that there is not a speck on my character."

CHAPTER II.

P EACE came, and with it a probable season of inaction ; but Nelson was not born for inactivity, and he had scarcely arranged his affairs after paying off the *Albemarle*, when he set out for France. His graphic description of his brief tour through the country, the object of whose darling ambition he was ordained afterwards to crush, is too interesting to be omitted :—

"On Tuesday morning, the 21st ult. [October, 1783], I set off from Salisbury Street, in company with Captain Macnamara of the navy, an old messmate of mine. I dined with Captain Locker, my old captain, at Malling, in Kent, and spent the night at his house. The next day we slept at Dover, and on Thursday morning we left England with a fine wind. In three hours and twenty minutes we were at breakfast in Monsieur Grandsire's at Calais. The quick transition struck me much. The manners, houses, and eating, so very different to what we have in England. I had thoughts of fixing at Montreuil, about sixty miles from Calais, on the road to Paris. We set off *en poste* they called it, but we did not get on more than four miles an hour. Such carriages, such horses, such drivers, and such boots, you would have been ready to burst with laughing at the ridiculous figure they made together. The roads were paved with stones ; therefore, by the time we had travelled fifteen miles, we were pretty well shook up and heartily tired. We stopped at an inn, as they called it,—a clean pigstye is far preferable. They showed us into a dirty room with two straw beds : they were clean, but that was all they could brag of. However, after a good laugh we went to bed, and slept soundly until morning. How different to what we had found the day before at Dover ! At daylight we set off, breakfasted at Boulogne, and got to Montreuil in the evening. This day we passed through the finest country my eyes ever beheld ; not a spot (as big as my hand) but was in the highest cultivation, finely diversified with stately woods. Sometimes, for two miles together, you would suppose you were in a gentleman's park. The roads are mostly planted each side with trees, so that you drive in almost a con-tinued avenue ; but amidst such plenty they are poor indeed. Montreuil is situated upon a small hill, in the middle of a large plain, which extends as far as the eye can reach, except towards the sea, which is about twelve miles from it. Game here was in the greatest abundance ; partridges, pheasants, woodcocks, snipes, hares, &c., &c., as cheap as you can possibly imagine,— partridges twopence-halfpence a brace, a noble turkey fifteen pence, and everything else in proportion. You will suppose that it was with great regret we turned our backs upon such an agreeable place ; but not a man that understood English, which was necessary to learn me French, could be found in the place. Our landlord at the inn is the same man that recommended Le Fleur to Sterne. From this place we proceeded on to Abbeville, ninety miles from Calais. This was a large town, well fortified ; but even there I could not be accommodated to my wish, nor indeed good masters, that is, that understand grammatically. At last I determined to come here [St. Omer], which, indeed, is what we ought to have done at first ; therefore, by the time we arrived, which was Tuesday week, we had travelled a hundred and fifty miles ; but on the whole I was not displeased with the excursion. This is by much the pleasantest and cleanest town I have seen in France. It is very strongly fortified, and a large garrison. We have good rooms in a pleasant French family, where are two very agreeable young ladies, one of whom is so polite as to make our breakfast for us, and generally, when we are at home, drink tea and spend the evening with us. I exert myself, you will suppose, in the French language, that I may have the pleasure of talking with them,—and French ladies make full as much use of their tongues as our English ones."

Nelson, in fact, became greatly enamoured of one of the young ladies, and made an offer of marriage, but which from prudential motives was declined. They were the daughters of an English clergyman, named Andrews, and a brother of the ladies, Lieutenant George Andrews, afterwards served under Nelson in the Mediterranean, and distinguished himself at the reduction of Bastia.

On returning to England, in March, 1784, Lord Howe, at that time First Lord of the Admiralty, gave our hero command of the 28-gun frigate *Boreas*, then lying in Long Reach, in the River Thames. He joined the ship in the month of March, superseding Captain Wells, and shortly afterwards quitted the river, bound to the Leeward Islands station. The *Boreas* having embarked Rear-Admiral Sir Richard and Lady Hughes and family (Sir Richard having been appointed commander-in-chief on the station), sailed from Spithead on the 19th of May. The voyage was a pleasant one. The ship was crowded with midshipmen, Nelson's kindness to whom attracted much attention from his passengers. Anxious to give the youngsters confidence in going aloft, it was his practice to race with them to the mast-head. At other times he superintended their studies ; and at noon was always the first to make his appearance, quadrant in hand. He never went on shore to pay visits of ceremony unaccompanied by a party of his youngsters.

Nelson being the senior captain on the station, was not long before he found himself involved in a series of professional combats against abuses and irregularities. On visiting Antigua, he found the *Latona* lying there bearing a broad pennant, and on inquiry found it to be that of Captain Moutray, resident commissioner at English Harbour. A written order was shown him, signed by Sir Richard Hughes, authorizing Captain or Commissioner Moutray to hoist a broad pennant on board any ship in the harbour. Nelson, knowing the order to be illegal—Captain Moutray holding no commission under the Admiralty, but a civil appointment—immediately sent an order to the captain of the *Latona* to haul down the broad pennant. He then went on shore and dined with the commissioner, to show that he had acted from no personal motive, but from a sense of duty. The case was referred to Sir Richard Hughes by Commissioner Moutray, and by Sir Richard to the Admiralty, and Nelson's act was approved. On another occasion, while lying at Nevis, a French frigate passed to leeward.

Upon inquiry he ascertained that the frigate had been despatched from Martinique, with engineer officers on board, to survey the British West India sugar-islands. Nelson was not long in putting to sea, and on the following day the *Boreas* anchored close upon the French frigate's quarter in St. Eustatia Roads. He met the French captain on shore at a dinner-party, at the Dutch governor's, when he took the opportunity of explaining very politely that he was aware of his (the French captain's) intention to visit the islands, and that he would with pleasure accompany him in the *Boreas* wherever he went. The French captain protested against giving Nelson so much trouble, which he said was quite unnecessary. Nelson, persevered in his politeness, until finding it impossible to evade such marked attention, the frigate returned to Martinique without accomplishing the object intended.

Nothing could escape his vigilance. The open infringement of the navigation laws, for which Nelson in common with most other British sailors had a profound respect, quickly took his attention. The Americans claimed, and were tolerated in the exercise of, the trading privileges of British citizens. The registers granted them previously to the separation of the two countries, were still held valid; and an occasional bribe administered to the fiscal authorities at once silenced all opposition. The question was, had the Americans forfeited their privileges with their allegiance to the Crown of Great Britain? If so, they were foreigners, and no longer entitled to trade upon the same terms as English citizens. Having satisfied himself upon this point, Nelson determined to act his part as a British sea officer. His *fidus Achates*, Collingwood, who commanded the *Mediator*, and Captain Wilfred Collingwood in the *Rattler*, joined heart and hand in the cause. The captains waited upon Sir Richard Hughes, called his attention to the Navigation Act, and after much persuasion obtained authority to put its provisions into execution. Armed with this authority Nelson went to Major-General Sir Thomas Shirley, Governor of the Leeward Isles, and told him how he was about to act. The old soldier ridiculed the youth of the captain, and told him he was not accustomed to take advice from young gentlemen. "Sir," replied Nelson, "I am as old as the prime minister of England, and quite as capable of commanding one of his majesty's ships as he is of governing the state."

While his affair was pending, Nelson was diligently engaged in paying his addresses to the widow of Dr. Nisbet. He was married to the lady on the 11th of March, 1787, Prince William Henry, then captain of the *Pegasus*, giving away the bride.

CHAPTER III.

THE period had now arrived which was to show Nelson in his true colours. Great in things of secondary importance, he was infinitely greater in affairs of moment. He had no longer to contend with litigious collectors of customs, and with a vacillating imbecile admiral. An enemy to the peace of the world was rising into power, and that enemy he was doomed, if not "to kill," at least to "scotch." It is worthy of remark, that the "little Corsican" and Nelson appeared to spring up simultaneously. It was at Toulon that Napoleon Bonaparte was first brought into notice, and it was at Toulon and Corsica that Nelson laid the foundation of future fame. It was at the birthplace of Bonaparte that Nelson gave such convincing proof of his superior ability.

On the 30th of January, 1793, Nelson was commissioned to the 64-gun ship *Agamemnon.* She was a fine ship of her class, and possessed very good sailing qualities. She was built in 1781, and had been in Rodney's celebrated action of the 12th of April, 1782. This was her second commission. The joy of Nelson was great at this unexpected change in his prospects, which a few weeks before had been all gloom. The *Agamemnon* was lying at Chatham, and thither he repaired, and hoisted his pennant on the 11th of February. He sent officers to the seaports of his native county to obtain volunteers, and many were the gallant fellows who hastened to obey the call. The popularity of Nelson caused his ship to be speedily and well manned. The *Agamemnon* arrived at Spithead

25

from Chatham on the 28th of April, and, after a short cruise in the Channel, sailed in Admiral Hotham's division of the Mediterranean fleet on the 11th of May. The fleet was under the command in chief of Admiral Lord Hood.

The ports of Toulon and Marseilles, and the fleet, had hitherto remained true to Louis. Negotiations were therefore entered into with the authorities, which ended in the town and fleets being provisionally placed in the hands of Lord Hood and Admiral Langara, in trust for the king of France. The result was, however, fatal to thousands of innocent people. The forts and harbour were retained until December, when the republicans prevailed. The dock-yard was burnt, and the shipping burnt or brought away, in which several thousands of fugitive royalists escaped. The remainder were murdered in cold blood by the monsters who obtained possession of the place. Nelson, however, had been despatched to Naples to communicate with the British envoy, Sir William Hamilton. It was here that he first became known to a syren, against whose allurements, unlike Ulysses of old, he was unhappily not wholly proof. Lady Hamilton was the most fascinating woman of her day—but we will not dwell upon this matter.

Having performed his mission to the court of Naples, and obtained, through Sir William Hamilton's influence, promises of 6,000 troops for the garrison of Toulon, Nelson sailed on the 29th of September, for Toulon, where he arrived on the 5th of October. On the 9th he received orders to proceed to Tunis, to join Commodore Linzee's squadron. On the 22nd, at 2h. A.M., being off Sardinia, and having only 345 men at quarters—the remainder having been landed at Toulon, the *Agamemnon* fell in with and chased the French frigate *Melpomene*, forty-four guns, 18 and 9-pounders, 400 men ; *Minerve*, same force ; *Fortunée*, 12 and 36-pounders, and 500 men ; a 24-gun corvette ; and a brig from Tunis. The enemy mistaking the *Agamemnon* for a frigate, allowed her to advance within shot of the sternmost—the *Melpomene ;* and a running action of three hours duration took place. The *Agamemnon* sustained much injury to her masts and yards from the frigate's well directed fire, and had one man killed and two wounded. Had the enemy's ships supported one another, the *Agamemnon* in all probability would have been captured. At 8h. A.M., however, showing no disposition to renew the action, and the *Agamemnon* being much disabled aloft, Nelson bore up for Cagliari to refit. The enemy appeared about noon to meditate an attack ; but finding the *Melpomene* so much damaged, they hauled up, and proceeded to Corsica.

Nelson joined Commodore Linzee at Tunis, and negotiations were entered into with the Bey, to induce him to withdraw his support from republican France, but in vain. From Tunis, Nelson was ordered by Lord Hood to proceed to Calvi, in Corsica, to co-operate with General Paoli and the anti-republican party in that island. Paoli, renowned in history as the great patriot of Corsica, had made overtures to Lord Hood. Commodore Linzee was also ordered to co-operate with the Corsican forces, and to endeavour to expel the French. St. Fiorenzo was attacked by Commodore Linzee, but the squadron was beaten off, chiefly by a martello tower, which set the engaging ships on fire by means of hot shot. This result was in part owing to Paoli's inability to make a simultaneous attack with his forces. Lord Hood having evacuated Toulon, brought his fleet to the attack. Lieut.-Colonel Moore (afterwards Sir John Moore) and Major Koehler, accompanied by Sir Gilbert Elliot, held a conference with Paoli, and it was agreed, that in the event of the expulsion of the French from Corsica, the island should be attached to the crown of England.

While this negotiation was pending, Nelson was cruising off St. Fiorenzo, where the French had erected a store-house containing flour near their only mill. Watching for a favourable opportunity, he landed a party of 120 men, who burnt the mill, threw the flour into the sea, and re-embarked without loss, although a thousand men were sent against him. The blockade of St. Fiorenzo was continued, and active measures taken to expel the French from the town and defences. This was at length effected through the united efforts of the soldiers and sailors—the latter of whom performed prodigies in dragging guns up almost inaccessible heights. The French sank three frigates at St. Fiorenzo, and retreated to Bastia.

It was now that Nelson's part became one of prominence. His bold offer to land and, with the seamen and marines of the squadron and such forces as Lord Hood could command, to take the almost impregnable citadel of Bastia, was such as must have startled the admiral himself. The journals which Nelson kept on the occasion, give by far the best account of the occurrences at that place :—

" March 1st.—Off Bastia.   2nd—Lord Hood in sight.   3rd.—Lord Hood
made my signal, and acquainted me of the retreat of our troops from the
heights, and of their return to St. Fiorenzo. Saw General Dundas's letter to
Lord Hood, as also Paoli's.   What the general could have seen to make a
retreat necessary, I cannot conceive. The enemy's force is 1,000 regulars, and
1,000 or 1,500 irregulars. I wish not to be thought arrogant, or presumptuously
sure of my own judgment ; but it is my firm opinion that the *Agamemnon*,
with only the frigates now here, lying against the town for a few hours, with
500 troops ready to land when we had battered down the sea-wall, would to
a certainty carry the place. I presumed to propose it to Lord Hood, and
his lordship agreed with me ; but that he should go to Fiorenzo and hear
what the general had to say, and that it would not be proper to risk having
our ships crippled without a co-operation of the army, which consists of
1,600 regulars and 180 artillerymen, all in good health, and as good troops
as ever marched.   We now know, from three Ragusan ships and one Dane,
that our cannonade on Sunday, the 23rd of February, threw the town into
the greatest consternation ; that it almost produced an insurrection ; that
La Combe St. Michel, the commissioner from the Convention, was obliged
to hide himself, for had he been found and massacred, to a certainty the
town would have been surrendered to me.   But St. Michel having declared
he would blow up the citadel with himself, was the only thing which prevented
a boat coming off to us with offers. A magazine blew up, and the people
believe we fired nothing but hot shot : the French shot were all hot.   That
by our cannonade on Tuesday afternoon, the 25th of February, the camp
was so much annoyed that the French ran, and in the town they so fully
expected I should land, that St. Michel sent orders for La Fleche to be burnt ;
but it falling calm, I could not lay near enough the town to do good service.
Many people were killed and wounded, and the master of the Ragusa, who
has been on board me, had a piece shot out of his leg, and the man next him
killed.   I lament that several women were killed, and a most beautiful girl
of seventeen. Such are the horrors of war. My ship's company behaved
amazingly well. They begin to look upon themselves as invincible—almost
invulnerable. I believe they would fight a good battle with any ship of two
decks out of France. Lord Hood offered me the *Courageux*, seventy-four,
but I declined it ; shall stay by *Agamemnon*.

"March 4th.—*Romney* joined. March 6th.—Close off Bastia ; the enemy adding strong posts for the defence of the place. At this moment Bastia is stronger than when our troops retired from it ; how that has hurt me. Received a letter from M. De Frediana to request an interview, provisions, powder, shot, flints, and, if possible, two cannon. Sent an officer overland to Lord Hood, with my opinion that it was yet possible to take Bastia with 500 regulars and two or three ships. Received a letter from Lord Hood to say he would send me two gun-boats according to my desire. When I get them, the inhabitants of Bastia sleep no more. Sent the *Romney* to Lord Hood.

"April 3rd.—Landed for the siege of Bastia. 4th.—At ten A.M. the troops, consisting of artillery and gunners 66 ; of the 11th regiment, 257 ; of the 25th, 123 ; of the 30th, 146 ; of the 69th, 261 ; of the marines, 218 ; and of chasseurs, 112 ; total 1,183 and 250 seamen, landed at the tower of Miomo, three miles to the northward of Bastia, under the command of Lieutenant-Colonel Villettes and Captain Horatio Nelson, who had under him Captains Anthony Hunt, Walter Serocold, and Joseph Bullen. At noon the troops encamped about 2,500 yards from the citadel of Bastia, near a high rock. The seamen and carpenters were all night employed in cutting down trees to form an abbatis and also to clear the ground towards the tower of Torga, whence the access to our camp was by no means difficult. A captain's picket was always mounted at Torga, with the sentry about a hundred yards in front of it.

" From April the 4th till the 10th, all the seamen were employed in making batteries and roads, and getting up guns, mortars, platforms, and ammunition-works, of great labour for so small a number of men, but which was performed with an activity and zeal seldom exceeded. On the 9th, about 11h. P.M., the enemy opened a very heavy fire upon our camp from their mortars and guns. The alarm was beat, and fully expected an attack. This firing lasted until daylight ; but not a single man was hurt. The tents were much damaged, but the troops being under arms, escaped.

"Lord Hood sent in a flag of truce on the 11th, at 7h. A.M., in one of the Victory's boats. The officer (Lieutenant Carré Tupper, of the Victory), on his landing was grossly abused, until the arrival o La Combe St. Michel, the commissioner for the Convention, when the mob became quiet. Having offered his letters to St. Michel, our officer was informed by the commissioner that he could not receive Lord Hood's summons,—' I have hot shot,' he exclaimed, 'for your ships and bayonets for your troops : when two-thirds of our troops are killed, I will then trust to the generosity of the English.' On the officer's return with this message, Lord Hood hoisted a red flag at the main-top-gallant masthead of the Victory, when our batteries opened upon the town, citadel, and redoubt of Camponella, the English colours having been hoisted on the rock over my tent, and every man giving three cheers. In our batteries were two 13-inch and two 10-inch mortars, one 8-inch howitzer, five 24-pounders, two 18-pounder carronades, three 12-pounders, one 4-pounder field-piece, distant from the redoubt of Camponella 800 yards, from the town battery 1,800, and from the centre of the citadel 2,300 yards. The enemy returned a heavy fire during the whole day. The *Proselyte* frigate anchored off the tower of Torga, about 1,200 yards from the town battery. Capt. Serocole, who commanded her, informed me that she took fire from red-hot shot, and that as he found the impossibility of getting the ship off the shore, he thought it right to set her on fire in several places, and she burnt to the water's edge.

   "April 12th.—A heavy fire was kept up by us during the whole of last night and this day, apparently with good effect, the enemy preserving a. continued fire upon us. In the afternoon I went with Colonel Villettes, Lieutenant Duncan, R.A., and Captain Clarke, brigade-major, with a Corsican guide, to examine a ridge about one thousand yards nearer the town than our present position, and on which the Corsicans kept a strong guard every night. The enemy's continued fire of musketry and grape was poured in on us during the whole evening. Unfortunately, the last shot that they fired from Camponella killed the Corsican guide, who was standing behind Clarke, and shot off his right arm and a part of his right side. Clarke was looking over my shoulder at Camponella, whence we were distant about 250 yards.

   "We began on the 13th of April a battery for three 24-pounders, close to the Torga tower, which stands on the sea-side, 1,230 yards from the town battery, and 1,600 from the citadel ; and a little in the rear a battery for two 24-pounders, a mortar battery for one 14-inch Neapolitan mortar, and for the two 10-inch mortars, which are to be removed from the upper battery. We were employed in getting up the guns, mortars, shells, shot, powder, and platforms, and in making the batteries until the 21st, as also a breastwork to cover 100 men in case of an attack.

"The Torga battery opened on the 21st of April, at daylight, on the town battery and Camponella, and apparently with good effect. The enemy kept up a most heavy fire on us the whole day with shells and shot from the citadel, town, Stafforella, Camponella, a square tower, and the two batteries newly raised under Stafforella. Brigadier-General D'Auban came on the heights from St. Fiorenzo with all the staff and field officers of that army, and a guard of fifty Corsicans.

"On the 3rd of May, we began a battery for one 24-pounder and a 10-inch howitzer, which was finished by the 7th, at night. The enemy, from the 1st of this month, had shown several dispositions, as if they meant to attack this post, but from some cause they never advanced. Five 4-pounder field-pieces, with good abattis, would, in my opinion, if the post had been well defended, have prevented their making any impression on it. The seamen always slept on the battery with their pikes and cutlasses.

"Lord Hood, on the 8th, sent in another flag of truce at eight o'clock, which was refused; the mayor telling the officer 'that they would return bomb for bomb, and shot for shot.' Opened the 24-pounder and howitzer with the greatest good effect; nor could all the efforts of the enemy knock down our works. A continued and increasing fire was kept up on the town and outworks. In the night of the 11th, a large boat came out of Bastia; she was closely pursued by our guard-boats and taken; in her were three deserters, the captain of La Fortunée frigate, twelve seamen, eight Corsicans, and thirty wounded soldiers, going to Capraja. Her despatches were thrown overboard, but in the morning of the 13th, at daylight, Lieutenant Suckling, of the St. Croix schooner, saw the packet floating on the water, which he took up and brought to me. Probably in the hurry of throwing them overboard, the weight that had been tied to them had slipped out of the string: they were all letters from Gentili, the commander-in-chief at Bastia, saying how much they had been annoyed by our fire, which had been opened on them near forty days, and that if succours did not arrive by the 29th of the month, they must look upon the town as lost to the republic.

"On the 22nd our troops, at 6h. P.M., marched from their posts, the
bands playing 'God save the king.' At 7h. the French colours were struck
upon Camponella, Stafforella, Croix de Capuchin, Monseratto rock, Fort
St. Mary's, and all the other outposts, and the British colours were hoisted
under three cheers from every seaman and soldier. The French troops all
retired to the town and citadel.   23rd.—This morning the British grenadiers
took possession of the town gates, and the gates of the citadel ; and on the
24th at daylight, the most glorious sight that an Englishman can experience,
and which, I believe, none but an Englishman could bring about, was
exhibited—4,500 men laying down their arms to less than 1,000 British
soldiers who were serving as marines.

" Our loss of men in taking Bastia, containing upwards of 14,000 inhabitants, and which, if fully occupied, would contain 25,000, was smaller than
could be expected.   Seamen killed and who died from their wounds, twelve ;
wounded, fourteen.   Soldiers killed and who died of their wounds, seven ;
wounded, twenty-three.   Total : killed, nineteen ; wounded, thirty-seven,
Officers wounded, Captain Rudsdale, of the 11th regiment, Captain Clarke,
of the 69th, and Lieutenant Andrews, of the *Agamemnon*.   By the most
accurate account we can get of the enemy's killed and wounded, they had,—
killed, 203, wounded, 540, most of whom are dead.   We consumed 1,658
barrels of powder, and fired 11,923 shot, and 7,373 shells."

" I am all astonishment," wrote Nelson, " when I reflect on what we have
achieved—4,000 men laying down their arms to 1,000 soldiers and marines,
and 200 seamen."   The force of the enemy was greater than he had
calculated upon, and at one time Nelson was under the impression that the
seige must be raised.   He, however, considered British honour to be at
stake, and he persevered until success at length crowned his efforts, and the
noble exertions of those by whom he had been supported.   Lord Hood
conveyed in the following letter his public thanks—his private acknowledgments were no less gratifying :—" The commander-in-chief returns his best
thanks to Captain Nelson, and desires he will present them to Captains
Hunt, Serocold, and Bullen, as well as to every officer and seaman employed
in the reduction of Bastia, for the indefatigable zeal and exertion they have
so cheerfully manifested in the discharge of the very laborious duties committed to them, notwithstanding the various difficulties and disadvantages

they had to struggle with, which could not have been surmounted but by the uncommon spirit and cordial unanimity that have been so conspicuously displayed, which must give a stamp of reputation to their characters not to be effaced, and will be remembered with gratitude by the commander-in-chief to the end of his life."

Intelligence having reached Lord Hood that the French fleet, having been repaired at Toulon and reinforced, had put to sea, his lordship determined to go in pursuit. The enemy's fleet had put into Gourjean Roads, where they were protected by powerful batteries ; but the approaches being too intricate, he was obliged to abandon the idea, once formed, of attacking them at the anchorage. The mode of attack proposed by Lord Hood, it is said, suggested to Nelson the plan of doubling on the enemy's van and centre, which plan he afterwards adopted at the Nile.

The *Agamemnon* and her now distinguished captain was next despatched to Calvi, to co-operate in the siege of that place with General Sir Charles Stuart. At this place Nelson was associated with an officer after his own heart. Though the projected employment was not less arduous than the siege of Bastia, Nelson now felt that he was serving with a general whose merits were great. The details of this siege are, however, of too much moment to be lightly dismissed, and we shall therefore resort to the journal kept by our hero on the occasion, which shows how difficult the undertaking was, and how ably the obstacles to success were surmounted

"June 13th.—Having ordered every transport and victualler, except the ships in the Mole, to be ready to sail with me, and a ship laden with empty casks, on the 13th of June, by eight o'clock, every soldier was embarked, amounting to 1,450 men, exclusive of officers. At noon made the signal to unmoor, and at four the signal to weigh. Sailed in company with the *Dolphin*, *Gorgon*, and twenty-two sail of vessels. At 7h. A.M. arrived at St. Fiorenzo, and anchored in Mortella Bay. General Stuart came on board, and expressed himself anxious to go on to the attack of Calvi, if I thought it right to proceed with the shipping, which I certainly did ; placing the firmest reliance that we should be perfectly safe under Lord Hood's protection, who would take care that the French fleet at Gourjean should not molest us. I therefore gave the necessary orders, and sailed the next day (the 16th), at 5h. 30m. P.M., from Mortella Bay, with the *Dolphin*, *Lutine*, and sixteen sail of transports, victuallers, and store-ships. It was 10h. P.M., on the 17th, before any of the ships could get to an anchor on the coast, about four miles to the westward of Cape Revellata, the bottom rocky, and very deep water ; the *Agamemnon* lying in fifty-three fathoms, about one mile from the shore, opposite a little inlet called Porto Agro. This coast is so rocky, except in this inlet, that a boat cannot land stores on any other place ; and it is with the greatest difficulty that a man can get up the cliffs.

" 19th.—The troops were disembarked at 7h. A.M., under the direction of Captain Edward Cooke, with six field-pieces, which the seamen dragged up the hills. I landed in the afternoon with 250 seamen, and encamped on the beach, getting on shore baggage for the army. By the general's desire I sent the *Fox* cutter, with directions for 180 of the Royal Louis, the 18th regiment, and 100 of the 69th regiment, to join as soon as possible. During the whole of the 20th and 21st it blew so strong, with a heavy sea and rain, and with such thunder and lightning as precluded all intercourse with the shipping, most of which put to sea. The seamen were employed in making wads for their guns, and in getting up three 24-pounders to the *Madona*, about two miles and a half from the landing-place, ready to act against Monachesco ; the road for the first three-quarters of a mile led up a steep mountain, and the other part was not very easy.

" On the 27th, we got up two 10-inch howitzers, and were employed all the day in carrying the heavy guns and carriages about three-quarters of a mile forward during constant rain. Throughout the whole time a gale of wind cut off all intercourse with the ships. At 1h. P.M. the French came out, and made an attempt to turn both flanks of the Corsicans. A gun-boat also came out to support their rear, and the enemy advanced under cover of a heavy cannonade. Our light corps were under arms to support the Corsicans if necessary, and the seamen got down two field-pieces and fired at the gun-boats, which instantly rowed away. The enemy rather forced our Corsicans to fall back, on which I went with General Stuart to them ; they kept up a smart firing of musketry, and regained their posts. Colonel Sabbatini, their commandant, was killed, with two or three others, and five or six wounded. The enemy retired to their works about 4h. P.M., and I believe have not the smallest idea of our intentions of bringing cannons over the mountains.

" July 3rd.—The seamen were employed for six hours in bringing up stores from the landing-place, and at night carrying casks, sand-bags, and platforms towards the intended battery. The French cannoniers and Royal Louis made the three-gun battery against Monachesco, which they are to have the fighting of.

" 4th.—The Royal Louis battery opened at daylight on Monachesco, and before evening did considerable damage to the enemy's works. It being the general's intention to make our battery this night against the *Mozelle*, he judged it proper to endeavour to draw off the enemy's attention from that place by a show of an attack on Monachesco. In the evening the Royal Irish marched from the right, whilst the light corps moved to the left. The Cosicans also, as soon as it was dark, began to fire, which the enemy think-ing to be an attack on Monachesco, fired in all directions, not only from the latter place, but from the *Mozelle*, Fountain battery, San Francesco, and the town. In a short time, thinking, I suppose, that we were in possession of Monachesco, they directed their cannon against it ; and their musketry was fired entirely across the isthmus, apprehending doubtless a general attack. It was General Stuart's orders, which were as plain as it was possible for orders to be, that the working parties should move forward with the sand-bags, casks, and platforms after sunset ; and as soon as they were got a little forward, I was to have moved with the guns ; but at 10h. 30m., when the general returned, not an engineer had advanced. An attempt, however, was made to erect the battery, but by midnight it was found im-possible to accomplish it and mount the guns before daylight. The general, therefore, ordered all the materials to be taken back to the place whence they had been brought.

" 5th.—Carrying junk for mortar platforms, and placing the mortars on their beds ; getting also things forward for the advanced battery. One hundred seamen were employed all night. Lieutenant Moutray made a battery for two 18-pounders inside Revellata, with twenty-five men.

" 6th.—Procuring some planks, and preparing everything to be ready to work briskly in the evening. At 9h. 30m. P.M. a feint of an attack was carried on against Monachesco, which succeeded amazingly well. Not a shot was fired at us, for the enemy turned their whole fire during the night towards the post which they imagined was attacked. By excessive labour,

and the greatest silence in every department, the battery was completed for
six guns within 750 yards of the *Mozelle*, and without the smallest annoy-
ance before daylight on the 7th, and the guns brought close to it ; but from
unavoidable circumstances, the guns could not be mounted on the platform
until two hours afterwards. The enemy did not fire at us until the fifth gun
was getting into the battery, probably never thinking of looking so near
themselves for a battery, when they opened a heavy fire of grape-shot on us :
but the seamen did their duty. Considering our very exposed situation, our
loss was small in numbers ; yet, amongst those who fell was Captain Walter
Serocold, of the navy, who was killed by a grape-shot passing through his
head, as he cheered the people who were dragging the gun. In him the
service lost a gallant officer, and a most able seaman. Three soldiers were
also killed, one of the *Agamemnon* s seamen, and Mr. Thomas Corney,
mate of the *Grand Bay* transport, who was one of the volunteers. A little
before six o'clock, we got two English 24-pounders and four 26-pounders
mounted on the platforms, in defiance of all opposition. At 10h. opened
our fire from this battery on the *Mozelle* and Fountain battery : not a gun
from the town can bear upon us, being so much covered by the *Mozelle*.
We also opened our hill battery of two 26-pounders and a 12-inch mortar,
1,500 yards from the *Mozelle*, with the Royal Louis battery of three 36-pounders
and two 12-inch mortars in the rear, and to the left of our advanced battery;
all which kept up during the whole day a constant fire on the enemy. At
3h. P.M. the enemy set fire to the façines in Monachesco, and abandoned
the post which the Corsicans took possession of. We had considerably
damaged the works by night, during which we fired occasionally on their
batteries. The enemy repaired much of their façine during the succeeding
night.

   " By ten o'clock on the 9th of July, we had evidently the superiority of
the fire, and before night had dismounted every gun in the Fountain battery
and *Mozelle* which bore upon us ; but the guns in San Francesco annoyed
us considerably, being so much on our left flank, and at so great a distance,
that we could not get our guns to bear on it with any effect. In the night,
we mounted the 10-inch howitzer 150 yards in the rear, and a little to the
left of our battery, both of which fired on the enemy every three minutes
during the night to prevent their working. Hallowell and myself each take*

twenty-four hours of the advanced battery. During this day one soldier was killed, and one soldier and two seamen wounded.

"At daylight on the 12th, the enemy opened a heavy fire from the town and San Francesco, which in an extraordinary manner seldom missed our battery ; and at seven o'clock, *I was much bruised in the face and eyes by sand* from the works struck by shot. The Mozelle was by this time much breached. At night replaced the guns destroyed, and fired a gun and mortar every three minutes. At half-past twelve the town was on fire, and burnt for three hours. We had two seamen and three soldiers wounded.

" During the whole of the 13th, a constant fire was kept up from the town, which struck our battery very often, and dismounted another 26-pounder. This is the fifth gun which has been disabled since the 7th, when our battery opened, and having only six guns in it, it is quite wonderful. At night we landed four 18-pounders, with a quantity of shot and shells in Port Vaccaja, and were employed in getting them up to the rear of our work ; and here I must acknowledge the indefatigable zeal, activity, and ability of Captain Hallowell, and the great readiness which he ever shows to give me assistance in the laborious duties that are intrusted to us. By computation to this night, we may be supposed to have dragged one 26-pounder with its ammunition, and every requisite for making a battery, upwards of *eighty miles, seventeen of which were up a very steep mountain.*

" 18th.—The 50th regiment were to assist in making a battery for three 26-pounders, to the right of the Mozelle, at about the distance of 300 yards ; the seamen were ordered to carry forward the guns and mount them, and also one 13-inch mortar. Sixty seamen, under Lieutenants Thomas Edmonds and George Harrison, were to carry forward the field-pieces. The disposition of the troops was as follows : Colonel Wemyss, with the 18th regiment, was to proceed by the left of our six-gun battery, with two field-pieces drawn by seamen, and with fixed bayonets was to take possession of the Fountain Battery, which having carried, the colonel was to direct his force against San Francesco, if it fired ; when the troops under Colonel Moore, with two field-pieces, drawn by seamen, were to move forward under cover of the three-gun battery, and carpenters under Lieutenant Thomas B. St. George, were to go before to cut down the palisades. A party under Major Brereton were to advance by the right of the Mozelle, and cut off the enemy's retreat from the town. Colonel Moore's party were to be supported by the 51st regiment; the 50th regiment, having finished their work at the battery, was to remain under arms ; and the troops were to move forward, lying on their arms. We continued all night hard at work, and landed 112 seamen from the *Agamemnon*, under Lieutenant Maurice W. Suckling.

" 29th.—The truce still continues ; at ten o'clock General Stuart went on board the *Victory*. At night four small vessels got into Calvi, and the garrison gave three cheers.   30th.—At noon an officer went into town with a flag of truce.   At 1h. 30m. he returned.   Got everything ready to recommence hostilities.   At 5h. 30m. began firing.   The garrison fired one general round, when they nearly all left their guns, only now and then stealing a gun at us.   By dusk three or four of their guns were totally disabled. During the night the enemy only fired three or four guns : we fired a gun every three minutes.   Lieutenant Byron, of the 18th Regiment, and Ensign Boggis, 51st Regiment, killed.   Lieutenant Livingstone, of the 30th Regiment wounded.   One seaman of the *Agamemnon* wounded.

"August 3rd.—A gale of wind all day.   The truce still continues.   4th, 5th, and 6th.—Gale continues ; still a truce.   7th.—Preparing transports to carry the garrison and inhabitants to France.   The gale abated.   8th.—Fine weather.   *Victory* and ships in sight.

"August 10th.—At nine o'clock, about 300 troops, a party of seamen, some Royal Louis, and some Corsicans, were drawn up opposite the great gate to receive the garrison of Calvi, who at ten o'clock marched out with two pieces of cannon and the honours of war ; amounting in the whole to 300 troops, and 247 armed Corsicans.   I immediately sent Lieutenant Montray, and a party of seamen, to take possession of the frigates, gun-boats, and merchant vessels in the harbour, and I also ordered six transports to come in ; and was employed all the day embarking the garrison, the sick, and such inhabitants as chose to return to France.   Out of their armed men the enemy had 313 sick in their hospital.   We have had six killed, six wounded, and two are missing.   We expended 11,275 shot and 2,751 shells. '

When placing this journal of his proceedings before his commander-in-chief, Nelson was not unmindful of the gallant officers and men by whom he had been so ably supported. "I have now only to acquaint your lordship," he wrote, "of the highly meritorious conduct of every officer and seaman landed under my command, and to express my sincere acknowledgments for the very effectual support and assistance I have received from the ability, zeal, and activity of Captain Benjamin Hallowell; and that Lieutenants Thomas Edmonds, James Morgan, and Ferrier, were constantly with the seamen fighting at the batteries, to which were joined on the last batteries Lieutenants Moutray, Joseph Hoy, and Maurice W. Suckling." Nelson also honourably mentioned Lieutenant George Harrison, agent for transports, and Mr. William Harrington, master of the *Wellington* and the crews of the transports.

Lord Hood, in addition to the high eulogium passed upon Nelson's conduct at Bastia, again bore testimony to his exertions at Calvi, and transmitted to England the journal which our hero had kept. But such was the loose way in which business was transacted at home, that his services, pre-eminent as they were, received no public notice. His name was not included among the wounded, a fact, however, which may be accounted for by the circumstance of his injury being by himself considered at the time as of little moment, and not officially returned. In referring to such brilliant services one can pardon the asperity on Nelson's part at such seemingly pointed neglect. "One hundred and ten days," said he, "I have been actually engaged at sea and on shore against the enemy; three actions against ships, two against Bastia in my ship, four boat-actions, and two villages, and twelve sail of vessels burnt. I have had the comfort to be always applauded by my commander-in-chief, but never rewarded." He concludes the sentence with the prophetic words, "I will have a gazette of my own."

The *Agamemnon* and the debilitated remains of her gallant crew now demanded attention. One hundred and fifty men were in their hammocks, fifty of whom died, and Nelson was ordered to Genoa for the double purpose of recruiting the health of himself and that of his crew, and of carrying despatches to Mr. Drake, the British minister of that place. The French had obtained possession of Vado Bay, and as it appeared probable they would attempt an invasion of Italy, Nelson was ordered to watch their movements.

Lord Hood, after the reduction of Corsica, quitted the Mediterranean for

England, leaving the fleet in command of Admiral William Hotham. Although Corsica was now a British possession, and under the charge of Viceroy Sir Gilbert Elliot, the state of the Mediterranean was not pro-mising. The Corsicans considered themselves a conquered people. Had England restored the island to Corsican rule, as an independent state, there seems little doubt that it would have remained so. By annexing it, however, to the crown of Great Britain, an opening was left for jealousy, and the French party were not long in undoing all that Lord Hood and his fleet had done. Tuscany had concluded a peace, and was at the mercy of France. Nothing but the British fleet preserved even a semblance of power in the Mediterranean, and that was threatened. A French fleet of seventeen sail of the line put to sea from Toulon, for the express purpose of testing British superiority. Admiral Hotham was at Leghorn with fifteen sail of the line, including the Neapolitan 74-gun ship *Tancredi* and the *Agamemnon*. We have Nelson's own narrative of the action which ensued.

The news of the fleet's being at sea was signalled by the *Mozelle* sloop on Sunday, the 8th of March. Admiral Hotham put to sea from Leghorn Roads on the morning of the 9th, but calms and light airs prevented any *recontre* until the morning of the 13th. Although in greater force than the British, Admiral Martin was evidently in doubt as to the working condition of his fleet, and declined rather than courted an engagement. Accident, however, rendered a partial action imperative. " On the 13th, at daylight," wrote Nelson, "the enemy's fleet in the south-west, about three or four leagues, with fresh breezes. Signal for a general chase. At 8h. A.M., a French ship of the line carried away her main and foretop-masts. At 9h. 15m. the *Inconstant* frigate fired at the disabled ship, but receiving many shot, was obliged to leave her. At 10h. tacked, and stood towards the disabled ship, and two other ships of the line. The disabled ship was the *Ça Ira*, of eighty-four guns, 36, 24, and 12-pounders, French weight; 42, 27, and 14-pounders, English weight, and 1,300 men; and the others, the *Sans-culotte*, 120 guns ; and the *Jean Barras*, seventy-four guns. We could have fetched the *Sans-culotte* by passing the *Ça Ira* to windward ; but on looking round I saw no ship of the line within several miles to support me ; the *Captain* was the nearest one on our lee quarter, I then determined to direct my attention to the *Ça Ira*, who, at 10h. 15m., was taken in tow by a frigate ; the *Sans-culotte* and *Jean Barras* keeping about gun-shot distance on her weather bow. At 10h. 20m. the *Ça Ira* began firing her stern chasers. At 10h. 30m. the *Inconstant* passed us to leeward, standing for the fleet. As we drew up with the enemy, so true did she fire her stern guns, that not a shot missed some part of the ship, and latterly the masts were struck by every shot, which obliged me to open our fire a few minutes sooner than I intended, for it was my intention to have touched his stern before a shot was fired. But seeing plainly, from the situation of the two fleets, the impossibility of being supported, and in case any accident happened to our masts, the certainty of being severely cut up, I resolved to fire so soon as I thought we had a certainty of hitting. At 10h. 45m., being within 100 yards of the *Ça Ira's* stern, I ordered the helm to be put a-starboard, and the driver and after-sails to be braced up and shivered, and as the ship fell off, gave her our whole broadside, each gun double-shotted. Scarcely a shot appeared to miss. The instant all were fired, braced up our after-yards, put the helm a-port, and stood after her again. This manœuvre we practised till 1h. P.M., never allowing the *Ça Ira* to get a gun from either broadside to bear on us. They attempted some of their after-guns, but all went far a-head of us. By this time the *Ça Ira* was a perfect wreck, her sails hanging in tatters, mizen-topmast, mizen-topsail, and cross-jack yards shot away. The frigate now hove in stays, and got the *Ça Ira* round. As the frigate first, and then the *Ça Ira*, got their guns to bear, each opened fire, and we passed within half-pistol shot. As soon as our after-guns ceased to bear, the ship was hove in stays, keeping, as she came round, a constant fire, and the ship was worked with as much exactness as if she had been turning into Spithead. On getting round, I saw the *Sans-culotte*, who had wore with many of the enemy's ships under our lee bow, and standing to pass to leeward of us, under top-gallant sails.

"At 1h. 30m. P.M., Admiral Hotham made a signal for the van ships to join him. I instantly bore away, and prepared to set studding-sails, but the enemy, having saved their ship, hauled close to the wind and opened their fire, but so distant as to do no harm—not a shot, I believe, hitting. Our sails and rigging are very much cut, and many shot in our hull between wind and water. But only seven men were wounded. The enemy, as they passed our nearest ships, opened their fire, but not a shot that I saw reached any ship except the *Captain*, who had a few passed through her sails. Till evening employed shifting topsails and splicing rigging at dark in our station ; signal for each ship to carry a light. Little wind, south-westerly all night ; stood to the westward, as did the enemy.

"At daylight on the 14th, taken aback with a fine breeze at N.W., which gave us the weather-gage, whilst the enemy's fleet kept the southerly gage. Saw the *Ça Ira*, and a line-of-battle-ship which had her in tow, about three and a half miles from us. The body of the enemy's fleet about five miles. 6h. 15m. A.M., signal for the line of battle S.E. and N.W. ; at 6h. 40m., for the *Captain* and *Bedford* to attack the enemy. At 7h. A.M. signal for the *Bedford* to engage close ; *Bedford's* signal repeated for close action ; 7h. 5m. for the *Captain* to engage close ; *Captain's* and *Bedford's* signals repeated. At this time the shot from the enemy reached us, but at a great distance. 7h. 15m. signal for the fleet to come to the wind on the larboard tack, but which was shortly afterwards annulled. This signal threw us and the *Princess Royal* to the leeward of the *Illustrious, Courageux,* and *Britannia.* At 7h. 20m. the *Britannia* hailed, and ordered me to go to the assistance of the *Captain* and *Bedford.* Made all sail. *Captain* lying like a log in the water, sails and rigging shot away ; *Bedford* on a wind on the larboard tack. At 7h. 40m. passed the *Captain,* hailed Admiral Goodall, told him Admiral Hotham's orders, and desired to know if I should go ahead of him. Admiral Goodall desired me to keep close to his stern. The *Illustrious* and *Courageux* took their stations ahead of the *Princess Royal.* The *Britannia* placed herself astern of me, and *Tancredi* lay on the *Britannia's* lee quarter. At 8h. the enemy's fleet began to pass our line to windward, and the *Ça Ira* and *Le Censeur* were on our lee side ; therefore, the *Illustrious, Courageux, Princess Royal* and *Agamemnon* were obliged to fight both broadsides. The enemy's fleet kept the southerly wind, which enabled them to keep their distance, which was very great ; from eight to ten engaging on both sides. About 8h. 45m. the *Illustrious* lost her main and mizen-masts ; at 9h. 15m. the *Courageux* lost her main and mizen-masts ; at 9h. 25m. the *Ça Ira* lost all her masts, and fired very little ; at 10h. *Le Censeur* lost her mainmast ; at 10h. 5m. they both struck. Sent Lieutenant George Andrews to board the prizes, who hoisted English colours, and carried the captains, by order of Admiral Hotham, on board the *Princess Royal,* to Admiral Goodall. By computation the *Ça Ira* is supposed to have had about 350 killed and wounded on both days ; and *Le Censeur* about 250 killed and wounded. From the lightness of the air of wind, the enemy's fleet and our fleet were a long time in passing. It was past 1h. P.M. before all firing ceased, at which time the enemy crowded all possible sail to the westward, our fleet lying with their heads to the S.E. and E." The casualties in the British fleet amounted to seventy-three killed, and 272 wounded, including Lieutenants Rathbone and Miles. Masters, Wilson, Blackburn, and Hawker.

Without claiming for Nelson a title more than his due, it is tolerably clear that but for his gallantry and skill in engaging the *Ça Ira*, nothing would have resulted from the desultory and indecisive movements, which for several days had marked the progress of the two fleets. Had not the *Agamemnon* fought the disabled French ship on the 13th, her damages might have been repaired. One crippled ship in a fleet acts as a general disability to the whole; and hence, as Admiral Martin could not leave the *Ça Ira* to fall a prey into the enemy's hands, the action on the 14th was unavoidable. Captain Fremantle, in the *Inconstant*, frigate, was among the first to attack the French fleet, and behaved nobly on the occasion.

Admiral Hotham was satisfied with his two trophies—not so Nelson. " Had we," said he, in a private letter, " taken ten sail and allowed the eleventh to escape, when it had been possible to get at her, I could never have called it well done." His advice was to leave the disabled *Courageux* and *Illustrious* with the prizes, and pursue the French fleet. Had his counsel been attended to, there can hardly be a doubt that the French fleet might then have been annihilated, as the ships were in a very disorganized state. " Sure I am," said our hero, when writing to his wife, " had I commanded on the 14th, that either the whole French fleet would have graced my triumph, or I should have been in a confounded scrape." That this was no idle vaunt, Aboukir, Copenhagen, and Trafalgar abundantly testify.

Southey and other biographers of Nelson have, we think, occasionally done much wrong to their hero, by placing the same stress upon his most confidential expressions as upon his publicly outspoken opinions. From this cause Nelson has been considered by many an egotist—a boaster; whereas nothing is more opposite to the truth. His public letters were such as a naval officer should write,—strong, vigorous, and to the point, but never arrogatory, and invariably giving honour to whom honour was due. But when writing to his wife or to a bosom friend, he gave utterance to his feelings unreservedly. Nothing is, we consider, more inexcusable than making such unguarded expressions the basis of Nelson's professional character. The reader cannot avoid acknowledging the truth of his criticisms upon the conduct of Admiral Hotham ; but had such insinuations been publicly mentioned, instead of being contained in a letter written to a wife (and Southey does not state to whom it was addressed), they would have been reprehensible. The thanks of Parliament were voted to the admiral, and the officers and men of the fleet.

Partial as the action was, it, for the time, saved Corsica ; but the blow was only parried for a brief interval. A reinforcement of six French sail of the line had, meanwhile, arrived at Toulon, while all Lord Hood's arguments in England could not induce the British government to despatch an efficient fleet to the Mediterranean. This lukewarmness caused Lord Hood to resign the command of the fleet, and his flag was hauled down in April, 1795, never to be rehoisted. A squadron of five sail of the line was, indeed, ordered to proceed to the Mediterranean, under the command of Rear-Admiral Man, but the reinforcement still left the British fleet inferior to the French.

Nelson received one gratifying mark of approbation by being, about this time, nominated a colonel of marines, and, which was still more agreeable, was ordered on detached service. The armies of Austria and Sardinia required the assistance and co-operation of a squadron, in order to drive the French from the Riviera di Genoa, and the *Agamemnon* and some frigates and small vessels were ordered to proceed to Vado Bay. But before reaching the scene of his intended operations, Nelson was in imminent danger of falling into the hands of the French fleet. On the morning of the 7th of July the *Agamemnon* was seen by Admiral Hotham's fleet, then lying in St. Fiorenzo Bay, under all sail returning to the bay, closely pursued and apparently surrounded by the enemy. Nelson's escape was a narrow one ; but the French fleet gave over the chase on observing the British fleet. Admiral Hotham immediately put to sea.

" We are now at sea," wrote Nelson, on the 8th of July, " looking for the French fleet, which chased myself and two frigates into Fiorenzo, yesterday afternoon. The admiral had sent me and some frigates to co-operate with the Austrian general in the Riviera di Genoa. When off Cape del Melle I fell in with the enemy, who, expecting to get hold of us, were induced to chase us over, not knowing, I am certain from their movements, that our fleet had returned into port. The chase lasted twenty-four hours, and owing to the fickleness of the winds in those seas, at times I was hard pressed ; but they being neither seamen nor officers, gave us many advantages. Our fleet had the mortification to see me seven hours almost in their possession ; the shore was our great friend, but a calm and swell prevented our fleet from getting out till the morning. The enemy went off yesterday evening, and I fear we shall not overtake them. If we have that good fortune, I have no doubt but we shall give a very good account of them, seventeen sail of the line, six frigates ; we twenty-three sail of the line, and as fine a fleet as ever graced the seas."

On the 14th he wrote : " Yesterday we got sight of the French fleet ; our flyers were able to get near them ; but not nearer than half gun-shot ; had the wind lasted ten minutes longer, the six ships would have each been alongside of six of the enemy. Man commanded us, and a good man he is in every sense of the word. I had every expectation of getting the *Agamemnon* close alongside an 80-gun ship with a flag or broad pennant ; but the west wind first died away, then came east, which enabled them to reach their own coast, from which they were not more than eight or nine miles distant. Rowley and myself were just cutting into close action when the admiral made our signals of recall. The *Alcide*, seventy-four, struck, but soon afterwards took fire by a box of combustibles in her fore-top, and she blew up. About 200 of her crew were saved by our ships. In the morning I was certain of taking their whole fleet, latterly of six sail. I will say no ships could behave better than our ships, none worse than the French ; but few men are killed ; but our sails and rigging are a good deal cut up. *Agamemnon*, with her usual good luck, had none killed, and only one badly wounded. By chance—for I am sure they only fired high—they put several shots under water, which have kept us ever since at the pumps. The enemy anchored in Frejus, and we are steering for Fiorenzo. The *Culloden* lost main-topmast as she was getting alongside a seventy-four." Nelson mentioned the *Victory*, Admiral Man ; *Captain*, Reeve ; *Agamemnon ; Defence*,

Wells ; *Culloden*, Troubridge ; *Cumberland*, Rowley ; *Blenheim*, Bazeley ; as the ships engaged on this occasion, but apologizes for any omissions.

After this brush, which took place off Hières islands—a battle it could not be called—Nelson proceeded to Genoa, having a squadron of eight frigates under his command.   In accordance with the advice of Mr. Drake, the British envoy, it was determined to stop the trade between France and Genoa, and the different places in the occupation of the French.   This, however, was attended with considerable risk, inasmuch as neutrals claimed certain privileges, to suspend which would render those who detained the vessels liable to civil actions.   Forewarned by experience and prudence, Nelson executed this delicate task with immunity to himself and the captains under him ; and he had the gratification of knowing he had put an end for the time to the fraudulent evasions of those traders under false colours.

General De Vins, with whom our hero had to co-operate, was old, timid, and consequently indecisive, and the whole work necessarily fell upon Nelson and his captains.   Spirited propositions fell upon an unwilling ear.   Had De Vins acted upon Nelson's suggestions, the supplies for the French army at Oneglia would speedily have been stopped, and Nelson at last entertained suspicions as to the sincerity of Austrian intentions.   "The army," said he, "is slow beyond all description ; and I begin to think the Emperor is anxious to touch another four millions of English money."   "War," he added, "is the trade of German generals, and peace their ruin ; therefore we cannot expect that they should have any wish to finish the war."   In anticipation that De Vins would lay the blame of the failure of his projected operations against Nice to the want of co-operation of the Sardinians and British, Nelson urged the general to state the time and place at which he wished to embark his troops.   To this De Vins replied, that as soon as Nelson was ready with vessels necessary for the transport of 10,000 men with their artillery and baggage, he would put the army in motion.   The general knew well that his demand was greater than could be complied with, and was thus enabled to reconcile himself to doing nothing.   Upon the whole, this service was most vexatious ; but Nelson had the gratification of finding his acts approved by his commander-in-chief.

On the 10th December, Nelson received orders to hoist his broad pennant on board the *Minerve* frigate, Captain George Cockburn, and, taking under his orders the *Blanche*, Captain Preston, proceed to Porto Ferrajo, to the assistance of the ships in that port, and to convey the troops and stores which had been landed there to Gibraltar and Lisbon. On his way to execute his mission, the Commodore fell in with two Spanish frigates. It was on the night of the 19th. The *Minerve* pursued the ship which carried a poop light, and the *Blanche* was ordered to go in chase of the other. At 10h. 20m. P.M. the *Minerve* brought the stranger to action, and after a smart running fight, which lasted till 1h. 30m. A.M., the enemy surrendered. The *Minerve's* opponent was the Spanish 40-gun frigate *Sabina*, Captain Don Jacobo Stuart. Previously to surrendering, the *Sabina* had her mizen-mast shot away and her fore and main-masts fell shortly after she struck. The *Minerve* had seven men killed, and Lieutenant Noble, Mr. Merry-weather, boatswain, and thirty-four wounded.

The *Blanche* did not succeed in overtaking the other frigate, *Ceres;* and at daylight she was discovered no longer the pursuer, but the pursued. Two Spanish line-of-battle ships and the *Ceres* were in eager chase ; and on discovering the *Minerve* and dismasted *Sabina*, they also became objects of attention. Lieutenants Culverhouse and Thomas M. Hardy, with a party of men, had been sent into *Sabina*. With unprecedented celerity they succeeded in getting up jury-masts, and in making sail upon the ship ; and it was mainly owing to the ability and able tactics displayed on board the *Sabina*, in diverting the Spanish squadron from her, that the *Minerve* was saved from capture. The *Minerve* reached Porto Ferrajo, where Nelson restored to the Spanish captain his sword, and sent him with a flag of truce, together with all the Spanish prisoners at Ferrajo, to Carthagena.

General De Burg, who commanded the garrison at Elba, scrupled about relinquishing his post without orders from England ; but Sir John Jervis's instructions were explicit, and Nelson, acting under his orders, withdrew the naval establishment, leaving the transports victualled, and ready to embark the stores and troops in three days. Before quitting the Mediter-ranean, Nelson received from Mr. Drake, the British envoy, the most gratifying testimony to the noble energy he had displayed on all occasions.

On the 22nd of January, 1797, the *Minerve* sailed from Porto Ferrajo, and proceeded to reconnoitre Toulon and Carthagena on her way to

Gibraltar. On the 1oth of February, he arrived at Gibraltar, where Nelson was happy to find the gallant lieutenants of the *Minerve* and the prize crew of the *Sabina*, who had been exchanged by the Spaniards. From Gibraltar he sailed for Lisbon, and only a few hours before the memorable victory off Cape St. Vincent, the *Minerve* joined Sir John Jervis's fleet. Nelson had learned some particulars repecting the Spanish fleet, which he was thus able to communicate, and Sir John immediately ordered him to rehoist his broad pennant on board the *Captain*.

At daylight on the 14th of February, 1797, a noble sight greeted the vision of Sir John Jervis and his brave followers: it was no less than a fleet of twenty-seven sail of the line, in two divisions, and in much disorder. The British fleet numbered only fifteen sail of the line, but included the imposing force of six three-decked ships. ·The Spanish admiral, in the weather division, was endeavouring to effect a junction with the lee division, consisting of nine sail, and Jervis determined to prevent this if possible. His fleet, in compact order on the starboard tack, close-hauled, was sufficiently advanced to frustrate the manœuvre ; and the Spanish admiral, finding that by persevering in his intention of crossing ahead of the fleet he would be obliged to engage the British with his ships in great disorder, wore round on the larboard tack, and bore away with the design of effecting a junction by going to leeward under the stern of the English line. Sir John Jervis now made the signal for his fleet to tack in succession. The *Culloden*, being the leading ship, was the first to obey the signal ; and that ship was soon blazing away at the rearmost Spanish ships. The *Culloden* was followed by the *Blenheim* and other ships astern ; but tacking in succession being a tedious process, it would have been a long time before it came to Nelson's turn, whose ship was stationed the third from the rear. Nelson, under the circumstances, put a very liberal construction on the order to tack and engage the enemy ; and observing, from his position in the line, the intention of the Spanish admiral, he determined to do his part towards frustrating the object. It must be clearly understood, that the leading Spanish ships were by this time abaft the weather beam of the *Captain*. Colonel Drinkwater, as well as Nelson, says the sternmost Spanish ships had done this, and the only way in which Nelson could take a part in the action was by wearing out of his position, and placing his ship across the bows of the enemy. He accordingly gave orders to Captain Miller to wear.

The order to wear was promptly obeyed, and by this bold and seemingly unauthorized evolution, Nelson was, in a short time, in the thickest of the fight. He engaged first the Spanish admiral, in the *Santisima Trinidad*— a huge four-decker of 136 guns, and continued his daring fight with a number of ships for a short time unassisted. The intrepid conduct of the commodore staggered the Spanish admiral, who already appeared to waver in pursuing his design of joining the ships cut off by the British fleet, when the *Culloden's* timely arrival, and Troubridge's spirited support of the commodore, together with the approach of the *Blenheim*, followed by Rear-Admiral Parker in the *Prince George*, with the *Orion*, *Irresistible*, and *Diadem* not far distant, determined the Spanish admiral to change his design altogether, and to throw out the signal for the ships of the main body to haul to the wind, and make sail on the larboard tack. Not a moment was lost in improving the advantage now apparent in favour of the British squadron. As the ships of Rear-Admiral Parker's division approached the enemy's ships in support of the *Captain* and her gallant seconds, the *Blenheim* and *Culloden*, the cannonade became more animated and impressive.

The *Captain* had by this time sustained the loss of her foretop-mast, and received such considerable damage in her sails and rigging, that she was almost disabled. The *San Nicolas* latterly had become the commodore's opponent. By the fire of this ship the *Captain* lost many men, and the damages already sustained through the long and arduous conflict which she had maintained appeared to render a continuance of the contest in the usual way precarious, if not impossible.

At this critical moment, Nelson resolved on a bold and decisive measure, and determined, whatever might be the result, to board his opponent. The boarders were summoned, and orders given to Captain Miller to lay the *Captain* on board the enemy. The order was judiciously obeyed, and the larboard bow of the *Captain* struck the starboard quarter of the *San Nicolas*, her spritsail-yard passing over the enemy's poop, and hooking in her mizen shrouds. When the order to board was given, the officers and seamen destined for this service, headed by Captain Edward Berry, together with the detachment of the 69th regiment, doing duty as marines on board the

Captain, commanded by Lieutenant Pierson, passed with rapidity on board the enemy's ship, and in a short time the *San Nicolas* was in possession of her intrepid assailants. The commodore's ardour would not permit him to remain an inactive spectator. He considered his presence might animate his brave companions, and contribute to the success of the enterprise ; he therefore accompanied the boarding party, by passing from the fore-chains of his own ship into the enemy's quarter-gallery, and thence through the cabin to the quarter-deck, where he arrived in time to receive the sword of the dying Commodore Geraldino, who had been mortally wounded by the boarders.

He had not long been employed in taking the necessary measures to secure this conquest, when he found himself engaged in a more arduous task. The *San Josef*, his former opponent, in consequence of her unmanageable state, had fallen on board the *San Nicolas*, the stern of that ship striking the weather-beam of the prize. The fire of musketry from the poop and galleries of this opponent having sorely annoyed Nelson's party, the commodore resolved as the best of two alternatives, to board the three-decker. Directing Captain Miller to send an additional number of men from the *Captain* on board the *San Nicolas*, Nelson headed the assailants in this new attack, exclaiming :—" Westminster Abbey, or glorious victory ! "

Success crowned the enterprise. The British no sooner appeared in the chains and on the quarter-deck of their new opponent than the commandant advanced, and asking for the British commanding officer, dropped on one knee, and presented his sword; apologizing, at the same time, for the Spanish admiral's not appearing, as he was dangerously wounded. Nelson could scarcely persuade himself of the reality of this second instance of good fortune. He ordered the Spanish commandant, who had the rank of a brigadier, to assemble the officers on the quarter-deck, and to direct means to be taken instantly for acquainting the crew with the surrender of the ship. The officers immediately appeared, and the commodore had the surrender of the *San Josef* duly confirmed, by each delivering his sword.

The coxwain of Nelson's barge had closely attended his commodore throughout this perilous movement. To him the swords of the Spanish officers were delivered as Nelson received them ; and the gallant tar tucked the honourable trophies under his arm with all the coolness imaginable. It was at this moment, also, that a British sailor, who had long fought under the commodore, came up in the fulness of his heart, and excusing the liberty he was taking, asked to shake him by the hand, saying, he "might not have such another place to do it in."

This conquest had scarcely been completed when the *San Nicolas* was discovered to be on fire in two places. At the first moment appearances were alarming; but the presence of mind and resources of Nelson and his officers n this emergency, soon got the fire under. A signal was now made by the *Captain* for boats to assist her clear from the two prizes ; and as she was incapable of farther present service, the commodore rehoisted his pennant on board the *Minerve* frigate. In the evening it was shifted to the *Irresistible*, Captain George Martin.

The " few remarks " subsequently written by Nelson must, of necessity, have a place in every history of the hero's performances :—"At 1h. P.M., the *Captain* having passed the sternmost of the enemy's ships, which formed their van and part of their centre, consisting of seventeen sail of the line, they on the larboard, we on the starboard tack, the admiral made the signal to tack in succession ; but perceiving all the Spanish ships to bear up before the wind, evidently with intention of forming their line, going large, joining their separated divisions—at that time engaged with some of our centre ships, or flying from us. To prevent either of their schemes from taking effect, I ordered the ship to be wore, and, passing between the *Diadem* and the *Excellent*, at a quarter past one o'clock, was engaged with the headmost, and, of course, leeward-most of the Spanish division. The ships which I knew were the *Santisima Trinidad*, 136 ; *San Josef*, 112 ; *Salvador del Mundo*, eighty ; *San Nicolas*, eighty ; another first-rate, and a seventy-four, names unknown.

" I was immediately joined and most nobly supported by the *Culloden*, Captain Troubridge ; the Spanish fleet not wishing, I suppose, to have a decisive battle, hauled to the wind on the larboard tack, which brought the ships above mentioned to be the leewardmost and sternmost ships in their fleet. For near an hour, I believe (but do not pretend to be correct as to time), did the *Culloden* and *Captain* support this apparently, but not really, unequal contest ; when the *Blenheim*, passing between us and the enemy, gave us a respite, and sickened the dons.

" At this time the *Salvador del Mundo* and *San Isidro* dropped astern,
and were fired into, in a masterly style, by the *Excellent*, Captain Collingwood, who compelled the *San Isidro* to hoist English colours ; and I
thought the large ship, *Salvador del Mundo*, had also struck ; but Captain
Collingwood, disdaining the parade of taking possession of a vanquished
enemy, most gallantly pushed up, with every sail set, to save his old friend
and messmate, who was to appearance in a critical state ; the *Blenheim*
being ahead, the *Culloden* crippled and astern.   The *Excellent* ranged up
within two feet of the *San Nicolas*, giving a most tremendous fire.   The
San Nicholas luffing up, the *San Josef* fell on board her ; and the *Excellent*
passing on for the *Santisima Trinidad*, the *Captain* resumed her station
abreast of them, and close alongside.   At this time, the *Captain* having
lost her foretop-mast, not a sail, shroud, nor rope left ; her wheel shot away,
and incapable of farther service in the line, or in the chase, I directed
Captain Miller to put the helm a-starboard, and, calling for the boarders,
ordered them to board.

" The soldiers of the 69th, with an alacrity which will ever do them credit,
and Lieutenant Pierson, of the same regiment, were almost the foremost in
this service.   The first man who jumped into the mizen chains was Captain
Berry, late my first lieutenant (Captain Miller was in the very act of going
also, but I ordered him to remain) ; he was supported from our sprit-sail-
yard, which hooked in the mizen rigging.   A soldier of the 69th regiment
having broken the upper quarter-gallery window, I jumped in myself, and
was followed by others as fast as possible. I found the cabin doors fastened,
and some Spanish officers fired their pistols ; but having broken open the
doors, the soldiers fired ; and the Spanish brigadier (commodore with a
distinguished pennant) fell, as retreating to the quarter-deck.   I pushed
immediately onwards for the quarter-deck, where I found Captain Berry in
possession of the poop, and the Spanish ensign hauling down.   I passed
with my people and Lieutenant Pierson, along the larboard gangway, to
the forecastle, where I met two or three Spanish officers, prisoners to my
seamen ;   they delivered me their swords.   A fire of pistols or muskets
opening from the admiral's stern-gallery of the *San Josef*, I directed the
soldiers to fire into her stern ; and, having placed sentinels at the different
ladders, called to Captain Miller, and ordered him to send more men into

the *San Nicolas*, and directed my people to board the first-rate, which was done in an instant—Captain Berry assisting me into the main-chains. At this moment a Spanish officer looked over the quarter-deck rail, and said they had surrendered. From this most welcome intelligence it was not long before I was on the quarter-deck, where the Spanish captain, with a bow, presented me his sword, and said the admiral was dying of his wounds. I asked him, on his honour, if the ship was surrendered; he declared she was; on which I gave him my hand, and desired him to call on his officers and ship's company, and tell them of it; which he did; and on the quarter-deck of a Spanish first-rate, extravagant as the story may seem, did I receive the swords of vanquished Spaniards; which, as I received, I gave to William Fearney, one of my bargemen, who put them, with the greatest *sang froid*, under his arm. I was surrounded by Captain Berry, Lieutenant Pierson, of the 69th regiment, John Sykes, John Thomson, Francis Cooke, all old *Agamemnons*, and several other brave men, seamen and soldiers. Thus fell these ships!

" N.B.—In boarding the *San Nicolas*, I believe we lost about seven men killed and ten wounded, and about twenty Spaniards lost their lives by a foolish resistance. None were lost, I believe, in boarding the *San Josef*. There is a saying in the fleet too flattering for me to omit telling, namely, ' Nelson's patent bridge for boarding first-rates,' alluding to my passing over an enemy's 80-gun ship."

The prizes to the British fleet, irrespective of those boarded by Nelson, were the 74-gun ships, *San Ysidro* (or *Isidro*) and *Salvador del Mundo.* Collingwood, in the *Excellent*, nobly assisted Nelson on this occasion. While the *Captain* was in close action with the *San Nicolas*, the *Excellent*, having received less damage, gallantly pushed between the *Captain* and her opponent, and, having cannonaded the Spaniard for some time, made sail in search of a fresh opponent. This memorable action terminated at 5h. P.M. The next day, the Spanish admiral having by that time effected a junction with the detached portion of his fleet, evinced a disposition to renew the engagement; but, observing the compact order of the British ships, changed his mind and hauled to the wind, leaving them in possession of the well-earned prizes.

In Sir John Jervis's brief public letter reporting the events of this decisive battle no particular mention was made of Commodore Nelson. This omission has been attributed by some writers to jealousy on the part of Sir Robert Calder, Sir John Jervis's flag-captain ; and by others to the fact of his having disregarded the admiral's signal to tack in succession. Another reason, and we think a more cogent one, seems to suggest itself. There were two vice-admirals and a rear-admiral whose flags were flying in the fleet, all of whom acted with commendable zeal and gallantry. The selection of Commodore Nelson for particular mention would, therefore, have been an indirect censure upon the flag-officers in the fleet ; and as it was notorious everywhere that Nelson was a kind of " pet " of the admiral's, the mention might have been attributed, with some show of reason, to partiality. Bearing in mind Nelson's subsequent acts, we are the more inclined to believe that it *was* Nelson who contributed mainly to compass the victory ; and doubtless the impulse he gave to the action by his unexpected evolution did much towards it. But the presence of one 74-gun ship could alone have availed little against seventeen thick-sided Spaniards. That Nelson acquitted himself in the noblest manner possible cannot for a moment be questioned, and his boldness in exercising his own judgment in such an emergency had at that time no parallel, and had none until he subsequently acted similarly on several important occasions. It is not, however, fair to the many brave officers and men who fought on board the *Culloden*, *Blenheim*, *Excellent*, *Prince George*, *Irresistible*, *Orion*, and other ships prominently engaged—not forgetting the *Victory* herself—to claim for the *Captain* an immoderate share of the laurels plucked on the 14th of February.

Recollecting the unfortunate issue of the 1st of June action, from Lord Howe's having mentioned certain ships more prominently than others, Sir John Jervis named no other officer than the captain of the fleet, Sir Robert Calder, whom he commended chiefly as the bearer of the despatches. In a private letter to Earl Spencer, First Lord of the Admiralty, Sir John wrote, —" The correct conduct of every officer and man in the squadron on the 14th instant, made it improper to distinguish one more than another in my public letter ; because I am confident, that had those who were least in action been in the situation of the fortunate few, their behaviour would not have been less meritorious." Upon the whole, however much Nelson might have felt aggrieved, he was not pointedly neglected, and suffered only in common with other heroes of the day, and probably more from inadvertence and haste than from any other cause.

The sword of the vanquished and deceased Spanish rear-admiral, which Nelson had received on board the *San Josef*, was tendered to Jervis, but the latter insisted on its being retained by the captor. Ever mindful of his native county, Nelson presented it to the city of Norwich, where it is to this day, together with the original letter which accompanied it, preserved in a glass case in the Town-hall of that city. For this action, Sir John Jervis was raised to the peerage ; the flag officers created baronets, and Commodore Nelson granted the order of the Bath, at that time a highly prized, because rare, distinction. Letters of congratulation poured in from all quarters. The public prints had made common the details excluded from the admiral's concise gazetted despatch, and Nelson's praises were upon every tongue. His venerable father's commendations were not the least touching :—"The height of glory to which your professional judgment, united with a proper degree of bravery, guarded by Providence, has raised you, few sons attain to, and fewer fathers live to see."

CHAPTER IV.

NELSON was now on the high road to fame. He had gained much more than all the Gazettings in the country could have given him—the admiration of the noble and the brave. There were some whose jealousy blinded them to the fact of his pre-eminence in his profession. There always have been, and ever will be, some—

"Who hate the excellence they cannot reach."

His commander-in-chief was not of the latter class. On Nelson's making his appearance on the *Victory's* quarter-deck, after the action, the admiral thanked him with unaffected cordiality, and in a most marked manner. Actions, however, are better than words—and the admiral did not fail to offer by his deeds unmistakable proofs of his just estimation of Nelson's valour and skill.

Our hero's commission as rear-admiral of the blue was dated the 20th of February, 1797 ; but information of the promotion did not reach him until April, when he was ordered to hoist his flag on board the *Captain*, and proceed to Porto Ferrajo to embark General De Burg and the garrison, at that place. On his return from this service, the important charge of the in-shore squadron off Cadiz was conferred upon him. He accordingly shifted his flag to the 74-gun ship *Theseus*, on the 24th of May, taking with him Captain Miller, and such officers as wished to accompany him, including

"Mids. Hoste and Bolton, &c., and such men as came from the *Agamemnon.*"

The crew of the *Theseus* had unhappily figured but a short time previously in a very insubordinate light ; Nelson, partly on that account, had been ordered to hoist his flag on board that ship, for his popularity among the seamen was undoubted. Shortly after the transfer, a letter was found on the quarter-deck, signed "the ship's company," containing the words, "Success attend Admiral Nelson! God bless Captain Miller. We thank them for the officers they have placed over us. We are happy and comfortable ; and will shed every drop of blood in our veins to support them ; and the name of the *Theseus* shall be immortalized as high as the *Captain's.*" The command which Nelson now enjoyed produced fighting enough to gratify the most gladiatorial disposition. Scarcely a night passed without an engagement with the Spanish gun-boats, launches, or batteries ; and Nelson's anxiety prompted him to be present in person on most occasions.

On the night of the 3rd of July, the launches of all the fleet, "without exception," armed each with a carronade, were ordered in-shore, together with the *Thunder* bomb, to attack Cadiz. The *Thunder* was judiciously placed ; and for a time her shells did good execution, but the largest mortar being disabled, she was ordered off. A number of Spanish armed launches and gun-boats having come out to drive away the British boats, some smart conflicts took place. Nelson's barge, as if by instinct, singled out that of the Spanish commandant, and, after some desperate fighting, the latter was captured. On this occasion, Nelson's life was saved by the devotion of the coxwain of his barge.

The noble conduct of John Sykes was mentioned by Nelson in his narrative of the boarding the *San Nicolas.* He on two occasions saved the life of Nelson by parrying the blows aimed at him, and at last actually interposed his own head, to receive the full force of a Spanish sabre ; which, fighting, as they were, hand to hand, he could not otherwise have prevented from falling on his admiral.

Nelson was now ordered on a service of great importance. Blake, in the time of the Commonwealth, by dint of sheer good fortune, made a successful attack upon some Spanish galleons in the bay of Santa Cruz, Teneriffe. Nelson, trusting to the same good fortune—which could alone have preserved him—failed. Intelligence had been received respecting the arrival at that place of the Spanish ship *El Principe d'Asturias*, from Manilla, bound to Cadiz with treasure and a valuable cargo. On the morning of the 14th of July, Sir Horatio weighed and stood towards the main body of the fleet, and at noon received orders to take under his command the 74-gun ships *Theseus, Culloden*, and *Zealous*, 50-gun ship *Leander, Seahorse, Emerald*, and *Terpsichore* frigates, *Fox* cutter, and a mortar-boat, and, by a sudden and vigorous assault, to attempt the town of Santa Cruz. Lord St. Vincent allowed Nelson to select such ships and officers as he approved from the fleet ; and when we add that the above-named ships were commanded by Captains Troubridge, Hood, Miller, Thompson, Fremantle, Waller, and Bowen, no one can doubt the wisdom of his choice. On Saturday the 15th, at 6h. A.M., this squadron, except the *Leander*, which had not then joined from Lisbon, but which followed him on the 18th, departed on their desperate mission.

On Sunday the 16th, the *Terpsichore* joined ; and on the 20th, when within thirteen leagues of Teneriffe, a general signal was made for the captains. Troubridge, of the *Culloden*, then received orders to take under his command the seamen and marines selected for the service, comprising 200 men of the *Theseus; Culloden*, 200 ; *Zealous*, 200 ; *Seahorse*, 100 ; *Terpsichore*, 100 ; *Emerald*, 100 : total 900, exclusive of commissioned officers and servants. Captains Hood, Miller, Fremantle, Bowen, and Waller were to command their several parties ; the marines were placed under Captain Thomas Oldfield, and a detachment of the Royal Artillery under Lieutenant Baynes. Captain Troubridge was also furnished with a formal summons, addressed to the governor or commanding officer of Santa Cruz. The summons demanded the immediate surrender of the town, batteries, and shipping, and stated the alternative to be the destruction of Santa Cruz and the levying a heavy contribution.

Everything which experience and caution could suggest was advised. On the afternoon of the 21st some further orders were issued :—"The *Culloden's* officers and men, with only their arms, to be ready to go on board the *Terpsichore* at 1h. P.M., to carry with them four ladders, each of which to have a lanyard four fathoms long, a sledge-hammer, wedges, and a broad axe. The boats' oars to be muffled either with a piece of canvass or kersey.'

Having received these orders, the captains went on board the frigates, and stood for Teneriffe.

The frigates, by twelve o'clock, had approached within three miles of the intended place of debarkation, but from the unforeseen circumstance of an adverse gale and a strong current, they were unable to get within a mile of the landing-place before the day dawned, which discovered the force to the Spaniards. At 3h. 30m. A.M., on the 22nd, the *Theseus* and squadron bore up for Santa Cruz, and at 4h. 30m. Nelson ascertained that the landing had not been effected.

On the 24th the ships were anchored about two miles to the northward of the town; and a disposition apparently evinced to attack the heights, which appeared to answer the end proposed. The *Leander*, Captain Thompson, joined in the afternoon, and her marines were added to the force before appointed, and Captain Thompson also volunteered his services. At 5h. 30m. P.M., the squadron anchored a few miles to the northward of Santa Cruz; and at six the signal was made for boats to prepare to proceed on service, as previously ordered. Nelson had now determined to conduct the enterprise in person; but before he left the *Theseus*, he addressed the following letter to Lord St. Vincent, the last he ever penned with his right hand:—" I shall not enter on the subject why we are not in possession of Santa Cruz; your partiality will give credit, that all has hitherto been done which was possible, but without effect; this night I, humble as I am, command the whole, destined to land under the batteries of the town, and tomorrow my head will probably be crowned with either laurel or cypress. I have only to recommend Josiah Nisbet to you and my country. With every affectionate wish for your health, and every blessing in this world, believe me, your most faithful, HORATIO NELSON." Nelson had a strong feeling that he should not survive the night, which accounts for the gloomy tone of his letter.

At 11h. P.M., the boats of the squadron, containing between 600 and 700 men, with 180 on board the *Fox* cutter, and about seventy or eighty in a boat taken the day before, proceeded in six divisions towards the town. The divisions of boats were conducted by their respective captains, except Fremantle and Bowen, who attended with the admiral to regulate and lead the way to the attack. Every captain had been made acquainted that the

landing was to be effected on the Mole, whence they were to hasten as fast
as possible into the great square, and there to form, and proceed on such
services as might be found necessary. The boats were not discovered until
1h. 30m. A.M., when, being within half gun-shot of the landing-place, Nelson
directed the boats to cast off from each other, give an huzza, and push for
the shore. The alarm-bells immediately rang, and a fire of thirty or forty
pieces of cannon, with musketry from one end of the town to the other,
opened upon the boats ; but nothing could stay the intrepidity of the
captains leading the divisions. Unfortunately, the night was extremely
dark, and the greatest part of the expedition did not see the Mole ; but went
on shore to the left of it, through a raging surf, which stove all the boats.
Captains Fremantle, Thompson, Bowen, and the admiral, with four or five
boats, found the Mole, which was instantly stormed and carried, although
defended by four or five hundred men. The guns—six 24-pounders—were
spiked ; but such a heavy fire of musketry and grape-shot was kept up from
the citadel and houses at the head of the Mole, that the British could not
advance. Nearly every man was killed or wounded.

Nelson's right elbow was struck by a musket-ball, as he was in the act of
drawing his sword and stepping out of the boat. This sword, which he had
so long and deservedly valued, from respect to his uncle, Captain Suckling,
was grasped in his left hand when falling, notwithstanding the agony he
endured. His step-son, Lieutenant Nisbet, who had remained close at hand,
saw his father wounded. He placed him at the bottom of the boat, and
observing that the sight of the quantity of blood which had flowed from the
shattered arm seemed to increase the faintness, he took off his hat to conceal
it. He then with great presence of mind examined the state of the wound,
and, holding the scattered arm so as to stanch the bleeding, took some silk
handkerchiefs from his neck, and tied them tightly above the lacerated
vessels. But for this precaution, Nelson, as he afterwards declared, must
have perished. Mr. Nisbet was assisted by John Lovel, one of the admiral's
bargemen ; who, having torn his shirt into shreds, constructed a sling for
the wounded arm. They then collected five other seamen, and with their
assistance got the boat afloat. Having succeeded thus far, Lieutenant
Nisbet took one of the oars that remained, and ordered the man who steered
to go close under the guns of the batteries, that they might be safe from

their tremendous fire. The voice of the lieutenant enforcing this judicious order roused Sir Horatio from his fainting state, and he immediately desired to be lifted up in the boat, that, to use his own words, "he might look a little about him;" he was accordingly raised by Nisbet. A painful uncertainty prevailed respecting the fate of his brave companions; and, on a sudden, a general shriek from the crew of the *Fox*, which had sunk from a shot she had received from the batteries, made the noble admiral forget his own weak and painful state. Many were rescued from a watery grave by the admiral's boat; and Nelson's exertions on the occasion, feeble though they were, added considerably to the agony and danger of his wound. Ninety-seven men, including Lieutenant Gibson, the commander, were lost, and eighty-three saved.

The first ship which the boat reached happened to be the *Seahorse;* but nothing would induce the wounded admiral to go on board, though he was assured that it might be at the risk of his life, if they attempted to row to another ship. "Then I will die!" he exclaimed; "for I would rather suffer death than alarm Mrs. Fremantle by her seeing me in this state, and when I can give her no tidings whatever of her husband." They proceeded without further delay for the *Theseus;* when, notwithstanding the increased pain and weakness from which he suffered, he peremptorily refused all assistance in getting on board. "Let me alone," he said; "I have yet my legs left, and one arm. Tell the surgeon to make haste and get his instruments. I know I must lose my right arm, so the sooner it is off the better."

Captain Fremantle was severely wounded in the right arm soon after the admiral, and, fortunately meeting with a boat on the beach, was taken on board the *Seahorse.* For the proceedings of Captain Troubridge and of the officers who were with him, Sir Horatio referred Lord St. Vincent to that officer's letter; and added, "I cannot but express my admiration of the firmness with which Captain Troubridge and his brave associates supported the honour of the British flag; and I must not omit to acquaint you with the satisfaction I received from the conduct of Lieutenant Baynes, of the Royal Artillery, not only from the ardour with which he undertook every service, but also from his professional skill."

Captain Troubridge's letter was dated *Culloden*, 25th:—"From the darkness of the night, I did not immediately hit the *Mole*, the spot appointed to land at, but pushed on shore under the enemy's battery, close to the southward of the citadel; Captain Waller landed at the same time, and two or three other boats. The surf was so high, many put back; the boats were full of water in an instant, and stove against the rocks, and the ammunition in the men's pouches was wet. As soon as I had collected a few men, I immediately advanced with Captain Waller to the square, the place of rendezvous, in hopes of there meeting you and the remainder of the people ; and I waited about an hour, during which time I sent a sergeant, with two gentlemen of the town, to summon the citadel. I fear the sergeant was shot on his way, as I heard nothing of him afterwards. The ladders being all lost in the surf, or not to be found, no immediate attempt could be made on the citadel; I therefore marched to join Captains Hood and Miller, who I had intelligence had made good their landing, with a body of men, to the south-west of the place I did. I then endeavoured to procure some account of you and the rest of the officers, but without success. By daybreak we had collected about eighty marines, eighty pike-men, and 180 small-armed seamen ; these I found were all who remained alive, that had made good their landing. With this force, having procured some ammunition from the Spanish prisoners we had made, we were marching to try what could be done with the citadel without ladders, when we found the whole of the streets commanded by field-pieces, and upwards of 8,000 Spaniards and 100 French under arms, approaching by every avenue. As the boats were all stove, and I saw no possibility of getting more men on shore, the ammunition wet, and no provisions, I sent Captain Hood with a flag of truce to the governor, to declare, ' I was prepared to burn the town, which I should immediately put in force, it he approached one inch farther;' and at the same time I desired Captain Hood to say, ' It would be done with regret, as I had no wish to injure the inhabitants ; that if he would come to my terms, I was willing to treat ;' which he agreed to. I had the honour to send you a copy of them by Captain Waller, which I hope will meet with your approbation, and appear highly honourable.

"The following parley was sent with the flag of truce :—'Santa Cruz, July 25th. That the troops, &c., belonging to his Britannic majesty shall embark with all their arms of every kind, and take their boats off, if saved, and be provided with such other as may be wanting: in consideration of which, it is engaged on their part, that they shall not molest the town in any manner by the ships of the British squadron now before it, nor any of the islands in the Canaries : and prisoners shall be given up on both sides.

" Given under my hand, and word of honour,

"SAM. HOOD."

" Ratified by T. TROUBRIDGE, and J. ANTONIO GUTIERREZ.' "

Captain Troubridge added, " From the small body of men, and the greater part being pike and small armed seamen, I could not expect to succeed in any attempt upon the enemy, whose superior strength I have before mentioned. The Spanish officers assured me they expected us, and were perfectly prepared with all the batteries and the number of men already mentioned under arms. This with the great disadvantage of a rocky coast, high surf, and in the face of forty pieces of cannon, will show, though we were not successful, what an Englishman is equal to ; and I have the pleasure to acquaint you that we marched through the town on our return with the British colours flying at our head.

" P.S.—I beg also to say, that when the terms were signed and ratified, the governor, in the handsomest manner, sent a large proportion of wine, bread, &c., to refresh the people, and showed every mark of attention in his power."

On the 27th, the surviving officers, seamen, and marines, were received on board their ships.

Captain Richard Bowen, who was killed in storming the Mole, was committed to the deep with the honours of war, and having paid the last melancholy duty to the remains of this gallant officer, Nelson sent off the following despatch to Lord St. Vincent, in the *Emerald*, Captain Waller, which sailed on the next day. " *Theseus*, off Santa Cruz. In obedience to your orders to make a vigorous attack on the town of Santa Cruz in the island of Teneriffe, I directed, from the ships under my command, 1,000 men, including marines, to be prepared for landing under the direction of Captain Troubridge, of H.M.S. *Culloden*, and Captains Hood, Thompson, Fremantle, Bowen, Miller, and Waller, who very handsomely volunteered their services ; and although I am under the painful necessity of acquainting you, that we have not been able to succeed in our attack, yet it is my **duty to** state, that I believe more daring intrepidity was never shown than by the captains, officers, and men you did me the honour to place under my command; and the detail which I transmit you herewith, will, I hope, convince you that my abilities, humble as they are, have been exerted on the present occasion. And among the former it is with the deepest sorrow I have to place the name of Captain Richard Bowen, of H.M.S. *Terpsichore*, than whom a more enterprising, able, and gallant officer does not grace his majesty's naval service ; and with much regret I have to mention the loss of Lieutenant John Gibson, commander of the *Fox* cutter, and a great number of gallant officers and men."

By the same conveyance the dejected Nelson sent the following pathetic communication to his admiral, dated *Theseus*, July 27th, 1797 :—

" I am become a burthen to my friends, and useless to my country ; but by my letter wrote the 24th, you will perceive my anxiety for the promotion of my son-in-law, Josiah Nisbet. When I leave your command, I become dead to the world ; I go hence, and am no more seen. If from poor Bowen's loss, you think it proper to oblige me, I rest confident you will do it; the boy is under obligations to me, but he repaid me by bringing me from the Mole of Santa Cruz. I hope you will be able to give me a frigate, to convey the remains of my carcase to England. God bless you, my dear sir, and believe me, your most obliged and faithful,

"HORATIO NELSON."

" You will excuse my scrawl, considering it is my first attempt."

Nelson's official leave was dated August 20th, and he sailed immediately afterwards in the *Seahorse*, and, on arriving at Spithead, received the Admiralty's permission on September 2nd to strike his flag. He proceeded without delay to his father and Lady Nelson at Bath. His letter, announcing the sad event, had not long preceded his arrival. "The difference of the hand-writing had at first perplexed the readers, and it was some time before Lady Nelson had discovered, with inexpressible anguish, that it was actually written by her wounded husband. They had heard of an expedition on which a part of Lord St. Vincent's fleet had been detached, and painful rumours had prevailed : neither of them had resolution to read it. The dreadful change in the well-known handwriting created an uncertainty, which magnified all that could have happened. At last Mrs. Bolton, who was on a visit to her father, at his request disclosed the contents ; she was sincerely attached to her brother, and for some minutes their affectionate sympathy rendered them insensible to the joy of his return. Whilst they were alternately expecting and despairing of his arrival, Lady Nelson one evening suddenly distinguished the sound of her husband's voice directing his carriage where to stop. The affectionate mind and filial regard of a son, so long absent, were rewarded by the blessings of an aged father, and by the tenderness of the faithful partner of his early and more humble fortunes."

During Nelson's sojourn at Bath, the freedom of the ancient city of Bristol . was transmitted to him by Mr. S. Worrall ; and he also received the freedom of the city of London. On the 22nd September, a letter from the Herald's Office reached him, signifying his majesty's gracious intention of investing him with the ensigns of the most honourable order of the Bath, and requesting his attendance at St. James's for that purpose on the 27th. Added to the honour of this order, his majesty's gracious manner, when investing him with its insignia, made a lasting impression. In such estimation did he hold this order, that he placed the numerous marks of distinction he subsequently acquired round the star of the Bath. This arrangement, however, occasioning an appearance of preference, was afterwards changed.

Previous to his leaving Bath, Lady Nelson had attended the dressing of his arm, until she had acquired sufficient skill and resolution to perform it herself, which she afterwards did continually.

As soon as his health was in some degree established, Nelson, with that devout sense which was so strongly impressed on his mind, went to the clerk of St. George's Church, and left with him the following paper :—" An officer desires to return thanks to Almighty God for his perfect recovery from a severe wound, and also for many mercies bestowed upon him. December 8th, 1797, for the next Sunday." It was the 13th before he was pronounced fit for service. He afterwards attended in the procession to St. Paul's on the 19th of the same month, when King George III. rendered public honour to the Supreme Being for the naval victories that had been gained.

3

It was not till the end of November that Nelson obtained any permanent relief from pain in his mutilated arm. After a night of sound sleep, a ligature, which could not before be removed without danger, came away at the slightest touch. From that time it healed, and his health was soon re-established. "Not having been in England," says Southey, "till now since he lost his eye, he went to receive a year's pay as smart-money; but could not obtain payment because he had neglected to bring a certificate from a surgeon that the sight was actually destroyed. A little irritated that this form should be insisted upon, because, though the fact was not apparent, he thought it was sufficiently notorious—he procured a certificate at the same time for the loss of his arm—saying, 'They might just as well doubt one as the other.' This put him in good humour with himself and with the clerk who had offended him. On his return to the office, the clerk, finding it was only the annual pay of a captain, observed he thought it had been more. 'Oh,' replied Nelson, 'this is only for an eye. In a few days I shall come for an arm; and in a little time longer—God knows—for a leg.' Accordingly he soon afterwards went, and, with perfect good humour, exhibited the certificate of the loss of his arm."

Sir Horatio being now convalescent, was not long in re-hoisting his flag. The *Foudroyant* was selected as his flag-ship, but not being ready in time, the *Vanguard*, seventy-four, was commissioned in the Medway for that purpose, on the 19th of December, 1797. It was not until March following, that the ship was ready for sea, and being at Spithead, Nelson's flag was once more displayed on the 29th. After several attempts to get clear of the Channel, the *Vanguard* at length started on the 9th of April, with a fair wind. After calling at Lisbon, the *Vanguard* joined Earl St. Vincent's fleet off Cadiz on the 30th. In a letter written by Earl Spencer, the First Lord of the Admiralty, to Earl St. Vincent, his lordship thus expressed himself in reference to Nelson:—

" I am very happy to send you Sir Horatio Nelson again, not only because I believe I cannot send you a more zealous, active, and approved officer, but because I have reason to believe that his being under your command will be agreeable to your wishes. If your lordship is as desirous to have him with you as he is to be with you, I am sure the arrangement must be perfectly satisfactory." To this St. Vincent replied, "I do assure your lordship that the arrival of Admiral Nelson has given me new life; you could not have gratified me more than in sending him; his presence in the Mediterranean is so very essential, that I mean to put the *Orion* and *Alexander* under his command, with the addition of three or four frigates, and to send him away the moment the *Vanguard* has delivered her water to the in-shore squadron, to endeavour to ascertain the real object of the preparations making by the French."

"It is ascertained," wrote Mr. Udney, the British Consul-general at Leghorn, to Nelson, "that 40,000 men will be embarked in at least 400 sail of vessels under General Bonaparte; their destinations are daily circulated and varied, so that no certainty can be obtained; but from all I can learn, by well-founded intelligence, I am confident their first attempt will be on Malta, thence to invade Sicily, in order to secure that granary; and then Naples; in all which places they have, by their emissaries, secured a strong party. What their other views afterwards may be with such an immense force, time will show; I, for my own part, am convinced that Bonaparte will pursue the scheme of seizing and fortifying Alexandria, Cairo, and Suez."

On the 28th of June Nelson and his fleet arrived off Alexandria, and the *Mutine* brig, Captain Hardy, was sent in to reconnoitre; but no French fleet had been seen or heard of. A course was then shaped for Caramania, and the fleet, under all sail day and night, coasted the southern side of Candia, working up against a strong wind. Nelson was in despair. He wrote letters accusing and excusing himself, and explaining all his reasons for acting as he had done. Baffled and dispirited, he proceeded to Sicily. It was now that, through the influence of Lady Hamilton, the wife of the British ambassador at the Court of Sicily, he obtained orders, addressed to the Sicilian authorities at Syracuse, to furnish the fleet with supplies. To this timely supply Nelson always attributed his ability to continue his successful pursuit. On the 25th of July Nelson sailed from Syracuse for the Morea, and entered the Gulf of Coron on the 28th. Here Troubridge ascertained that the French fleet had been seen steering south-east from Candia. To Alexandria, therefore, Nelson again directed his course, and on the memorable 1st of August, at noon, gained sight of the Pharos tower.

The bay was now no longer deserted, but crowded with shipping ! Nelson's anxiety up to this time had been such as to deprive him of sleep and appetite. His mind had been upon the rack ; but he was now satisfied that the enemy, of which he had been so long in search, was within his grasp.   He ordered dinner to be served, at which most of his officers were present ; and when his guests rose from the table to repair to their several stations, he said to them emphatically : "Before this time to-morrow I shall have gained a peerage, or Westminster Abbey."

He had resolved to divide his fleet into three squadrons, in the following manner :—

Vanguard,	*Orion,*	*Culloden,*
Minotaur,	*Goliath,*	*Theseus,*
Leander	*Majestic,*	*Alexander,*
Audacious,	*Bellerophon.*	*Swiftsure.*
Defence,		
Zealous.		

Of these squadrons, two were to attack the ships of war, while the third was to pursue the transports.   The soundness of his plan must be obvious to every capacity, and no doubt can be entertained that, had circumstances occasioned it to be put into execution, the success would have been signal.

The evening preceding the action, the *Alexander* and *Swiftsure* had been detached ahead, to reconnoitre the harbour of Alexandria, while the rest of the squadron remained in the offing.   The enemy's fleet was first discovered by the *Zealous,* Captain Hood, who communicated by signal the number of ships at anchor, in line of battle, in the Bay of Aboukir. The *Vanguard* instantly hauled to the wind, a movement that was observed and quickly followed by the whole squadron, and at the same time Nelson by signal recalled the *Alexander* and *Swiftsure.*

We must now proceed to the battle itself.   There was no chart of the coast in the fleet ; and to get at the enemy was the difficulty.   The Bay of Aboukir commences about twenty miles E. N. E. of Alexandria, and extends from Aboukir Castle, situated at the northern point or headland, in a deep curve as far as the western mouth of the Nile, distant from the castle about six miles.   This bay has not sufficient depth of water for large ships nearer to the shore than three miles—a long sand-bank, on which there is only twenty-four feet of water, extending to that distance. About two miles N.E. by E. from Aboukir Castle is Bequier Island (Nelson's Island it is now called), and from this a bank or reef extends nearly two miles farther out to sea, in a north-easterly direction. The French ships, with their heads to the westward, were moored in line, or rather in a very obtuse angle, at the centre of which was the French admiral's ship *L'Orient.* The ships ahead and astern of the admiral were about 160 yards apart, and the headmost about two miles distant from Aboukir Castle. Beginning from the headmost ship, the following was their order in the line of battle :— *Guerrier*, 74 ; *Conquérant*, 74 ; *Spartiate*, 74 ; *Aquilon*, 74 ; *Peuple Souverain*, 74 ; *Franklin*, 80 ; *Orient*, 120 ; *Tonnant*, 80 ; *Heureux*, 74 ; *Timoléon*, 74 ; *Mercure*, 74 ; *Guillaume Tell*, 80 ; *Généreux*, 74. The frigates *Diane*, *Justice*, *Artémise*, and *Sérieuse*, two brigs, and several gunboats, were moored in-shore. The British fleet consisted of thirteen sail of the line, one of fifty guns, and the *Mutine* brig.

At 3h. P.M. Nelson made the signal to prepare to anchor, and at 4h. to anchor by the stern, for which purpose cables were passed out of the gun-room ports, and bent on to the anchors at the bows. At 5h. 30m. the signal was made to form in line ahead and astern of the admiral, as most convenient, and the *Zealous* was ordered to lead the fleet. As usual, however, under such circumstances, each ship kept the leads constantly going, carefully sounding. Captain Foley, by the better sailing of his ship, had now gained the honour of leading. The evening was serene, the water smooth, and the sun, making "a glorious set," cast a rich flow over the scene.

A light breeze of wind from N.W. wafted the ships slowly down upon the enemy. At 6h. 20m. the French fleet hoisted their colours. The *Guerrier* and *Conquérant*, aided by the battery on Aboukir Island and the gun-boats, now opened fire upon the leading British ships. It was Captain Foley's intention to anchor on the in-shore bow of the *Guerrier*, but some delay in letting go the anchor obliged him to bring up farther in advance, and abreast the *Conquérant* on the inside. As the *Goliath* passed ahead of the *Guerrier* she poured in a heavy raking fire. Hood observing the cause of the *Goliath* not bringing up in the intended place, immediately ordered the

Zealous's anchor to be dropped, and that ship occupied the *Goliath's* n-
tended position on the bow of the *Guerrier.* The fall of the *Guerrier's*
fore-mast, which no doubt the *Goliath's* fire had contributed to occasion, was
the first sight to greet the British fleet. The *Audacious* was the first to
anchor in accordance with the admiral's orders, and brought up about fifty
yards from the *Conquérant's* starboard or off-shore bow. The *Theseus* went
inside and anchored by the stern, abreast the *Spartiate;* and the *Orion,*
following the *Theseus,* anchored by the head inside, a little abaft the beam
of the *Peuple Souverain.* The *Sérieuse* frigate having fired at the *Orion,*
one broadside was returned from the effects of which she almost immediately
sank.

The *Vanguard* was the next ship to anchor, and as she anchored outside,
it seems a sufficient proof that this was the admiral's plan. The *Vanguard*
brought up by the stern outside the *Spartiate,* distant not more than eighty
yards from her starboard beam. All the ships, by a standing order of Earl
St. Vincent, wore the St. George's ensign. This flag was used more particularly, the better to distinguish the English from the French ensign ; the
flag of which being blue, might otherwise be mistaken for English. Each
ship was decked with union jacks on the top-mast stays. The *Minotaur*
anchored ahead of the *Vanguard,* and, fortunately for the latter, outside
the *Aquilon,* whose previously destructive fire upon the *Vanguard* was thus
diverted. The *Bellerophon* anchored close alongside the *Orient,* 120, and
the *Majestic* on the starboard-side of the *Tonnant.* The *Swiftsure* was
unable to get into action till 8h. P.M., by which time the *Bellerophon* had
been dismasted, and was drifting out of the action, and the *Swiftsure* took
up a position a little on the bow of the *Orient.* The *Leander* having been detained by endeavouring to assist the *Culloden* off the shoal, arrived about
the same time, and anchored most judiciously ahead of the *Franklin.* The
Alexander, having been despatched to look out, was the last in ; that ship
anchored on the starboard-quarter of the French admiral.

We must now return to the *Vanguard.* In a few minutes, owing to her
having to sustain a raking fire from the *Aquilon,* the men stationed at the
six foremost guns fell as fast as the guns could be remanned. The *Minotaur,*
however, as we have just stated, arrived very seasonably, and took off the
Aquilon's destructive fire. The fight now raged with awful fury. The

French rear, by Nelson's well-devised plan, although unengaged, could not get up to the assistance of the van and centre, and in consequence, the whole of the latter were soon reduced to wrecks, and five surrendered.

In the heat of the battle, Nelson was struck on the forehead by a piece of langridge, and, in an instant, was blinded by the blood and loose flesh, which fell over his eye. The stunning sensation caused him to stagger, and he would have fallen, had not Captain Berry caught him in his arms. It was thought that he had been shot through the head. He was immediately conducted below to the cockpit, which, by this time, was crowded with the wounded. The surgeon, Mr. Jefferson, naturally solicitous for his admiral's state, hurried to Nelson; but he desired him to wait until his (the admiral's) turn came. The pain was excruciating, and he considered it to be mortal. He, therefore, desired the chaplain, Mr. Comyn, to attend him, and delivered him an affectionate message for Lady Nelson; and ordered a commission to be made out for Captain Hardy, in the room of Captain Berry, whom he intended sending home with the despatches. He felt so grateful to Captain Louis for having so nobly supported him, that, at about 9h. P.M., he directed Lieutenant Capel to go on board the *Minotaur* in the jolly-boat, and desire Captain Louis to come to him, that he might thank him for his conduct; adding, "this is the hundred and twenty-fourth time I have been engaged, but I believe it is now nearly over with me." Captain Louis hastened on board the *Vanguard*, and the meeting which took place between them was most affecting. Providence, however, had determined to preserve Nelson for other triumphs. When the surgeon had examined the wound, it was found to be not mortal; and the intelligence quickly circulated throughout the ship, to the great joy of all.

About 8h. 30m., the *Aquilon* and *Peuple Souverain* were taken possession of, and Captain Berry sent a lieutenant and a party of marines for the same purpose to the *Spartiate*, which ship had struck to the *Vanguard*. The officer brought back the French captain's sword, which Captain Berry immediately took below to the admiral. The victory was now decisive, for although the *Heureux*, *Tonnant*, and *Orient* were not taken possession of, they were silenced, which intelligence Captain Berry had likewise the satisfaction of communicating in person to the admiral.

A few minutes after nine, the French admiral's ship was discovered to be on fire in the mizen chains, and was soon enveloped in flames. The French admiral had heroically sustained the honour of his flag, but, at length, a cannon-ball cut him asunder. He had previously received three desperate wounds, one on the head, and two in his body, but could not be prevailed upon to quit the deck. Commodore Casa Bianca fell by his side. Several of the officers and men, seeing the impracticability of extinguishing the fire, which had now extended itself along the upper decks, and up the masts, jumped overboard. The British did their utmost to save their fellow-creatures, now no longer enemies.

The *Swiftsure*, being within half pistol-shot of the larboard bow of *L'Orient*, saved the lives of the commissary, first lieutenant, and ten men, who were drawn through the lower-deck ports. The situation of the *Alexander* and *Swiftsure* became extremely perilous. The looked-for explosion of such a ship was an event to be guarded against. Captain Hallowell, however, refused to move from his station, though repeatedly urged to do so. He perceived the advantage he possessed in being to windward of the burning ship. The *Alexander*, having twice taken fire, was under the necessity of shifting her berth, and moving to a greater distance.

The admiral was informed by Captain Berry of the situation of the enemy. Forgetting his own sufferings, he scrambled on deck ; and his first thought was that of concern for the lives of his late enemies. He ordered Captain Berry to make every exertion in his power. A boat, the only one that would swim, was despatched from the *Vanguard*, in command of Lieutenant Edward Galway ; the other ships followed the example, and above seventy poor fellows were preserved. The moon, which had by this time risen, added to the grandeur and solemnity of the picture. The flames had made such progress that an explosion was instantly expected ; and at 9h. 37m. the flames reached the magazine, and the ship blew up with a crashing sound that deafened all around. The tremulous motion, felt on board each ship, was like that of an earthquake. A death-like pause of about three minutes ensued, before the fragments, driven to a vast height into the air, could descend. A port-fire fell into the main-royal of the *Alexander*, and set it on fire ; but the flames were soon extinguished. Two burning fragments of the wreck likewise dropped into the main and fore-tops of the *Swiftsure*, but without causing serious injury.

Silence reigned for several minutes, as if the contending squadron, struck w th horror at the dreadful event, which in an instant had hurled so many brave men into eternity, had forgotten their hostile rage, in pity to the sufferers. The *Franklin*, bearing the flag of Rear-Admiral Blanquet, who had become senior officer, was the first to recommence the action. The *Swiftsure*, being now free from her late formidable adversary, had leisure to direct her whole fire into the quarter of the *Franklin;* and in a short time, by the well-directed fire of the *Swiftsure* and *Defence*, assisted by the *Leander*, the *Franklin* was compelled to call for quarter.

The *Alexander*, *Majestic*, and occasionally the *Swiftsure*, were now the only British ships engaged ; but Captain Hallowell, finding that he could not direct his guns clear of the *Alexander*, which had dropped between him and the *Tonnant*, desisted, although still severely annoyed by the shot of the *Tonnant*. The firing ceased at about 3h. A.M. on the 2nd ; but, just as the day dawned, the *Alexander* and *Majestic* recommended the action with the *Tonnant*, *Guillaume Tell*, *Généreux*, and *Timoleon*. The *Heureux* and *Mercure* had fallen out of the line, and had anchored a considerable distance to leeward.　　　　　　　　　　　　　　•

Eight ships had now surrendered, and the *Heureux* and *Mercure* were captured by the *Goliath* and *Theseus* on the succeeding day. The *Timoleon*, but with her colours flying, was on shore ; and about two miles from that ship was the *Tonnant*. The latter ultimately surrendered, on the 3rd, to the *Theseus* and *Leander;* but the *Timoleon*, after hauling down her colours, was set on fire by her own crew, who escaped to the shore. Two line-of-battle ships and two frigates out of this fine fleet escaped—the *Généreux*, *Guillaume Tell*, *Diane*, *Justice;* and it is worthy of remark that three of these were eventually captured by a squadron under Lord Nelson's command. The damages of the British fleet, with the exception of the *Bellerophon*, were chiefly confined to the masts and rigging. The *Bellerophon*, from having taken up her berth on the broadside, instead of the bow or quarter of the *Orient*, was dreadfully shattered in hull, and totally dismasted.

Nelson, in whose mind a sense of Providential care was always observable if not paramount, now evinced his gratitude to the great Arbitrator of events. On the morning of the victory he issued the following memorandum to the captains of his ships—one only of whom, Captain Westcott, had perished in the fight :—

> " *Vanguard*, off the Mouth of the Nile,
> 2nd day of August, 1798.

"Almighty God having blessed his majesty's arms with victory, the admiral intends returning public thanksgiving for the same at two o'clock this day, and he recommends every ship doing the same as soon as convenient."

" To the respective captains of the squadron."

Accordingly, at 2h. P.M., divine service was performed on the quarter-deck of the *Vanguard*, by the Rev. Mr. Comyn. The other ships followed the example of the admiral, though perhaps not all at the same time. This solemn act of gratitude to Heaven seemed to make a deep impression on many of the prisoners, and some were heard to remark, "that it was no wonder the English officers could maintain discipline and order, when it was possible to impress the minds of their men with such sentiments, after a victory so great, and at a moment of such confusion."

A victory more complete, and more important in its consequences, had never graced the annals of the British navy. Out of a fleet of seventeen sail, four only escaped capture or destruction. The bold nature and originality of the attack could only be rivalled by the persevering courage with which it was supported, and the unparalleled success with which it was crowned. For a week after the battle the Bay of Aboukir was covered with the bodies of the slain—a most painful and horrid spectacle ; and although men were continually employed in sinking the bodies with shot, yet the shot having slipped off, many re-appeared upon the surface. Considering the heat of the weather, it was surprising that no pestilential disorder broke out, in consequence, among out gallant countrymen.

The captains of the British fleet—the band of brothers, as Nelson called them—vied with each other in sending various presents made from the wreck of the *Orient*, to the hero under whose auspices this signal victory had been achieved. Among the number Captain Hallowell, of the *Swiftsure*, ordered his carpenter to make a coffin from the wood and iron of the wreck. The carpenter accordingly finished one with considerable elegance, from the main-mast of the ill-fated ship, and it was subsequently presented to the admiral with the following note :—

" My Lord,—I have taken the liberty of presenting you a coffin made from the main-mast of *L'Orient*, that when you have finished your military career in this world, you may be buried in one of your trophies ; but that that period may be far distant is the earnest wish of your sincere friend,

" BEN. HALLOWELL.

" *Swiftsure*, May 23rd, 1799."

The enthusiasm excited by the event, it would defy more than any ordinary descriptive power to display. The Grand Seigner sent Nelson a pelisse of sables with broad sleeves, valued at 5,000 dollars, and a diamond aigrette, estimated at 18,000 dollars. These magnificent presents were accompanied by a purse of 2,000 sequins, to be distributed among the wounded. The mother of the sultan sent a box set with diamonds, valued at £1,000. The Czar Paul presented a gold box containing his portait, set in diamonds. The king of Sardinia, who had so short a time before refused the rights of hospitality to the weather-beaten squadron, also sent a gold box studded with diamonds. The honours awaiting his arrival at Naples were boundless. In England the effects of the victory were astounding. News of the first fruitless chase had reached, and blame was laid to the charge of Lord St. Vincent for sending so young an admiral on so important a service. But now the story was changed. He had gained the peerage and escaped Westminster Abbey, and on the 6th of October became Baron Nelson, of the Nile, and of Burnham Thorpe, in the County of Norfolk.

The sword of Rear-Admiral Blanquet was intrusted to Captain Capel, to be presented to the city of London, with an appropriate letter to the Lord Mayor.

On the meeting of Parliament, in the month of November, his Majesty, in opening the session, by a speech from the throne bore the most flattering testimony to Nelson's high deserts :—" The unexampled series of our naval triumphs has received fresh splendour from the memorable and decisive action, in which a detachment of my fleet, under the command of Rear-Admiral Lord Nelson, attacked and almost destroyed a superior force of

the enemy, strengthened by every advantage of situation. By this great
and brilliant victory, an enterprise, of which the injustice, perfidy, and
extravagance, had fixed the attention of the world, and which was peculiarly
directed against some of the most valuable interests of the British empire,
has in the first instance been turned to the confusion of its authors ; and
the blow thus given to the power and influence of France has afforded an
opening which, if improved by suitable exertions on the part of the other
powers, may lead to the general deliverance of Europe." Shortly afterwards
a message from the king was presented to the House of Commons by Mr.
Pitt, to the following effect :—" His Majesty, having taken into his serious
consideration the signal and glorious victory obtained by Rear-Admiral
Lord Nelson over a superior force of the enemy, in the action off the Mouth
of the Nile, on the 1st of August last, not only highly honourable to himself, but singularly beneficial to the interests of these kingdoms ; and being
desirous to bestow a signal and lasting mark of his favour on the said
Admiral Lord Nelson, did grant unto him, the said Admiral Lord Nelson,
an annuity of two thousand pounds per annum. But his Majesty not pos-
sessing the means of continuing the same, nor having it in his power to
secure it to the said Lord Nelson beyond his own life, recommends it to his
faithful Commons to make such provisions as to them should appear fit, to
enable his Majesty to carry his intentions into effect." Mr. Pitt thereupon
moved, " that a pension of two thousand pounds per annum, to commence
on the first of August, 1798, should be granted to Admiral Lord Nelson, of
the Nile, and his two next successors in the title." General Walpole, who
seconded this motion, thought that Lord Nelson should also have a higher
degree of rank. Mr. Pitt, in reply, observed, that, " entertaining the highest
sense of the transcendent merits of Admiral Nelson, he thought it needless
to enter at any length into the question of rank. His fame must be coeval
with the British name ; and it would be remembered that he had obtained
the greatest naval victory on record, when no man would think it worth his
while to ask whether he had been created a baron, a viscount, or an earl."
Mr. Johnes declared that in his opinion the consequences of Lord Nelson's
achievement were such as to entitle him to the appellation of the saviour
of mankind.

    Nelson, in the midst of his successes, which would be sure to make him new ones, was thoughtful of his old friends. He appointed Mr. Alexander Davison, whom he first knew in the West Indies, sole prize-agent for the captured ships ; and Davison, not to be outdone in a question of generosity, ordered gold medals to be struck commemorative of the glorious event, which he presented to the different captains ; the same in silver for lieutenants and warrant-officers ; in gilt metal for petty officers ; and in copper for seamen and marines. This act of patriotism cost Mr. Davison £2,000. These medals were actually the only testimonials in existence recording the Nile action until 1848, when it was included among the battles entitling the survivors to the silver naval medal.

CHAPTER V.

LADY HAMILTON—NELSON DRIVES THE FRENCH FROM NAPLES—
IS MADE DUKE OF BRONTE.

1798—1800.

" I DETEST this voyage to Naples," wrote Nelson to Earl St. Vincent, two days before reaching the bay; " nothing but absolute necessity could force me to the measure. On the day Hoste left me I was taken with a fever, which has very nearly done my business: for eighteen hours my life was thought to be past hope. I am now up, but very weak both in body and mind, from my cough and this fever. I never expect, my dear lord, to see your face again: it may please God that this will be the finish to that fever of anxiety which I have endured from the middle of June: but be that as it pleases His goodness—I am resigned to His will." In this depressed, yet proper frame of mind, Nelson now entered upon an entire new act in the drama of his life. Esteemed as he had been by all to whom he was known, but that chiefly among his brother officers and immediate friends, he had never had to perform the part of a great man on shore till now. " On the 22nd," he wrote, " the wreck of the *Vanguard* arrived in the Bay of Naples. His Sicilian majesty came out three leagues to meet me, and directly came on board. His majesty took me by the hand, and said such things of our royal master, our country, and myself, that no words I could use would in any degree convey what so apparently came from the royal heart. From his majesty, his ministers, and every class, I am honoured by the application of ' Nostro Liberatore.' " This interesting letter, evidencing

78

the pure sentiments of Nelson's heart in the midst of a vortex of flattery, proceeds: "You will not, my lord, I trust, think that one spark of vanity induces me to mention the most distinguished reception that ever, I believe, fell to the lot of a human being; but that it is a measure of justice due to his Sicilian majesty and the nation. If God knows my heart, it is amongst the most humble of the creation, full of thankfulness and gratitude!"

Previously to his arrival, he also wrote to Lady Nelson: "The kingdom of the two Sicilies is mad with joy; from the throne to the peasant, all are alike. According to Lady Hamilton's letter, the situation of the queen was truly pitiable. I only hope I shall not have to be witness to a renewal of it. I give you Lady Hamilton's own words:—'How shall I describe the transports of the queen! "'Tis not possible," she cried, kissed her husband, her children, walked frantically about the room, cried, kissed and embraced every person near her, exclaiming, " O, brave Nelson! O, God bless and protect our brave, brave deliverer. O, Nelson, Nelson, what do we not owe to you? O victor! Saviour of Italy! O, that my swollen heart could now tell him, personally, what we owe to him!"' You may judge, Fanny, of the rest; but my head will not allow me to tell you half: so much for that. My fag, without success, would have had no effect; but blessed be God for His goodness to me."

Public demonstrations of joy were loud, but apparently sincere. The liberty of Italy had, without doubt, for the time been preserved from the French yoke. Not less flattering were the private marks of attention paid to him. In his letter to Lord St. Vincent, Nelson did not mention the fact that Lady Hamilton accompanied his Sicilian majesty ; but in a letter to his wife he wrote: " Sir William and Lady Hamilton came out to sea, attended by numerous boats and emblems, &c. They, my most respectable friends, had really been laid up, and seriously ill: first from anxiety, and then from joy. It [the news of the late action] was imprudently told Lady Hamilton in a moment, and the effect was like a shot; she fell apparently dead, and is not yet recovered from severe bruises. Alongside came my honoured friends ; the scene in the boat was terribly affecting ; up flew her ladyship, and exclaiming, ' O, God ! is it possible !' she fell into my arm more dead than alive. Tears, however, soon set the matter to rights, when alongside came the king. I hope, some day, to have the pleasure of introducing you to Lady Hamilton ; she is one of the very best women in the world : she is an honour to her sex. Her kindness, with Sir William's, to me, is more than I can express ; I am in their house. Lady Hamilton intends writing to you."

Few readers will, unhappily, be so thoroughly unacquainted with the world as to place implicit confidence, as Nelson appears to have done, in the sincerity of this demonstration on the part of Lady Hamilton. She was an accomplished actress, and in this, as in almost all other passages of her life, expressed very much more than she felt. The naïve description of her conduct given by Lord Nelson, however, clearly shows that he had not penetration enough to discover the secret spring of her actions, or to attribute this conduct to the right motive—that of building her own fortunes at the Neapolitan court upon Nelson's acts and fame. Lady Hamilton was at this time a most fascinating woman, and doubtless made a very serious inroad upon Nelson's amicable affections ; but we cannot admit that there was at this time anything criminal in the passion. Lady Hamilton, in fulfilment of her promise, wrote to Lady Nelson on the 2nd of December ; but before the letter reached, some injurious reports appear to have forestalled upon its contents. Lord Nelson's most intimate friend, Mr. Davison, writing to him on the 7th of December, said : " I cannot help again repeating my sincere regret at your continuation in the Mediterranean ; at the same time I would be grieved that you should quit a station, if it in the smallest degree affected your own feelings. You certainly are, and must be, the best and only judge : yet you must allow your best friends to express their sensations. Your valuable and better half writes to you. She is in good health, but very uneasy and anxious. . . . Lady Nelson this moment calls, and is with my wife. She bids me say that unless you return home in a few months, she will join the standard at Naples. Excuse a woman's tender feelings—they are too acute to be expressed." Nelson, however, must have been either a most unprincipled (a supposition not consistent with his character) or an injured man. Writing to Lady Nelson, between the 1st and 6th of October, probably at the very moment when these suspicions were entertained, he says, " The Grand Seignor has ordered me a valuable diamond ; if it were worth a million, my pleasure would be to see it in your possession. My pride is in being your husband—the son of my dear father, and in having Sir William and Lady Hamilton for my friends."

But to return from this digression, Nelson found himself involved in a perfect labyrinth of gaiety. All the arts which could be brought to bear to enliven and delight the great hero, the liberator of Italy, were employed. His birthday, which happened a week after his arrival, was celebrated in a most splendid *fête*. But the mummeries and gaieties fell coldly upon his heart—he could see through the flaunting garb of folly and weakness. "What precious moments the court of Naples and Vienna are losing!" he exclaimed. "Three months would liberate Italy; but the court is so enervated, that the moment will be lost. I am very unwell, and their miserable conduct is not likely to cool my irritable temper. It is a country of fools and fiddlers, scoundrels, &c." If ever for a moment he was blinded by the displays of this court, or seduced by its blandishments, the illusion was but transitory. He saw through all a mass of treachery and iniquity, and the real miseries under which the country was groaning. A system of barefaced corruption and infamous favouritism prevailed throughout the court. Ferdinand and his queen mingled with thoughtless licentiousness the most perfect unconcern for the people; and provided the revenue of the kingdoms which was to administer to their gratification was raised, they heeded little what means were employed in its collection.

The defeat of Bonaparte's fleet had shut him up with his army in an arid desert, and the various European powers, emboldened by the successes of the British arms, rallied their forces, and determined to re-assert their independence. Russia, Austria, and now Naples mustered their troops. Naples, after great persuasion, in which Lady Hamilton's influence with the queen had much weight, consented to join the coalition with a force of 80,000 men. Nelson did not hesitate to impress upon the king that he had no alternative between being kicked out of his kingdom or being prepared to die sword in hand. At the urgent desire of the court, Nelson consented to remain at Naples instead of going to Alexandria to destroy the transports. The royal family desired the squadron as a guarantee for their personal safety, and as the means of escaping from the malice and vengeance of their enemies.

The first point at which Nelson aimed was the recovery of Malta, to which island his Neapolitan majesty alleged he had a claim. A rigorous blockade was established by Captain Ball; but the resources and strength of the island were more than he could surmount. The island of Gozo, however, was taken possession of in the name of his Sicilian majesty, by the squadron under Nelson's personal superintendence. The *Vanguard* returned to Naples on the 5th of November, in company with the *Minotaur*.

General Mack was in command of the Neapolitan troops. "All that is now doubtful concerning this man," says Southey, "is whether he was a coward or traitor." The result proved him to be very much of both. While Mack, at the head of 32,000 men, marched into the Roman states, the British and a Portuguese squadron, under the Marquis de Niza, embarked 5,000 troops, aud proceeded to take possession of Leghorn. The latter object was effected without opposition. The Grand Duke of Tuscany, disgusted by the treatment received from the French authorities, came readily into the proposed surrender. But the Neapolitan general, Naselli, refused to seize the French vessels in the port, disregarding the fact of the conquest of Gozo, and alleging that the King of Naples was not at war with France. Awed by the threats and arguments of Nelson, Naselli at length agreed to place an embargo on the French vessels. These included several privateers, and about seventy sail of vessels of Liguria— under which name Genoa had now become a republic. The latter being laden with corn for Genoa and France, would have been of great assistance to the troops, and would have enabled more to enter Italy. Nelson had the whole weight on his shoulders. The Neapolitans—more than half-traitors—were his unwilling supporters ; but he did not give up the point until the crews of the privateers were sent away and the corn landed from the Genoese shipping. Having completed this affair so far satisfactorily, he wrote to Mr. Wyndham : "I am content ; the enemy will be distressed, and I shall get no money. The world, I know, think money is our god ; and now they will be deceived as far as relates to us."

On the 30th of November, Nelson quitted Leghorn for Naples. Complimentary addresses of every description were showered down upon him on his arrival—and an Irish Franciscan, among other things, prophesied that Lord Nelson would take Rome with his ships. When told of the impossibility of his prophecy, he notwithstanding boldly adhered to his affirmation. But a cessation of this tide of eulogy was now about to take place. The King of Naples was with the army at Rome, but the French occupied the castle of St. Angelo, and 13,000 French troops were posted at Castellana. Mack marched against them with 20,000 fine young men. Upon his success hung the fate of Naples. Nelson anticipated the result. "The Neapolitan officers," in a letter dated the 11th December, to Earl Spencer, said Nelson, "have not lost much honour, for they had but little to lose; but they lost all they had." General St. Philip, commanding the right wing, consisting of nearly 9,000, fell in with 3,000 of the enemy near Fermi, and, after a little distant firing, deserted to them. One of his sergeants, possessed of some sense of honour, levelled a musket at the renegade, and shot him through the arm. He joined the French, however, and pursued with them the troops he had lately betrayed. The route was complete—cannon, tents, baggage, and military stores were taken.

Ferdinand returned to Naples, and every day brought tidings of some other reverse. The feeling in the city was such, that neither Sir William Hamilton nor Lord Nelson could appear at court; their every movement was watched, and a plan was formed by the revolutionary party to seize and detain them as hostages, to prevent the town from being fired upon after the French should have taken possession. "There is an old saying," wrote Nelson to Earl Spencer, "when things are at the worst they must mend; now the mind of man cannot fancy things worse than they are here; but thank God, my health is better, my mind never firmer, and my heart in the right trim to comfort, relieve, and protect those whom it is my duty to afford assistance to."

Everything had, meanwhile, been arranged, chiefly by Lady Hamilton, for the removal of the royal family from a place where their lives were no longer safe. The danger of the operation was considerable; the mob and the lazzaroni were attached to the king, and relying on their numbers and strength, insisted upon his remaining with them. In this dilemma, a sub-terranean passage leading from the palace to the sea-shore was explored by Lady Hamilton, through which by degrees, a great portion of royal treasures, paintings, sculptures, and property amounting in all to two millions and a half, were conveyed away and shipped off. On the night of the 21st of December, at half-past eight, Nelson landed and escorted the whole royal family in three barges. A heavy sea was rolling into the bay, but the whole got off in safety to the *Vanguard*. Notice was then given to the British merchants that they would be received on board any ship of the squadron, their goods having been previously embarked on board transports. Two days were passed in the bay, waiting for those who chose to avail themselves of the opportunity, and on the 23rd the fleet got under way for Sicily, leaving orders with the Marquis de Niza to destroy the Neapolitan ships of war. A gale came on next day ; one of the princesses died in Lady Hamilton's arms, and during all the passage, that lady attended upon her royal friends with the most zealous care. On the 26th the *Vanguard* reached Palermo.

The flight of the royal family to Palermo had not been premature, for Prince Pignatelli, who had been left as vicar-general and viceroy, with orders to defend the kingdom to the last extremity, immediately sent plenipotentiaries to the French camp before Capua, and it was ultimately agreed, on the 10th of January, 1799, to sign an armistice, by which the greater part of the kingdom was yielded up to the enemy. The French advanced towards Naples, when the traitor Mack, under the pretence of being sheltered from the revenge of the lazzaroni, deserted to General Championet, by whom he was forwarded, under an escort, to Milan ; but hoping for his further services, he was considered a prisoner of war. The lazzaroni alone remained true—the Neapolitan officers, troops and all, having dispersed and disbanded. Every post was defended with desperate courage by the lazzaroni. Undaunted by the strength of their enemy, they resisted to the last extremity ; and it is supposed they would have rendered Naples untenable, had one man of genius and true courage been present to direct their energies. In order finally to overcome the resistance of this body, the French had recourse to the priests ; and a miracle—one of those bleeding impostures—of St. Januarius, produced a partial calm. The French obtained possession of Naples, and the next day '' Te Deum '' was sung by the archbishop in the cathedral.

The Austrian cabinet appeared to regard the conquest of Naples very lightly, and used no effort to avert the further extension of the French rule. The King of Sardinia, driven by the exactions of the French to extremities, at length put himself under British protection. Tuscany was soon added to French dominion, and Nelson entertained apprehensions for Sicily. His representations upon this latter subject were not disregarded. Sir

Charles Stuart, and 1,000 men, hastened thither from Minorca. Had this assistance not arrived, however, Nelson would have defended Messina with his naval force alone. Upon the whole, Nelson was placed in a position perhaps the most difficult and perplexing that can be imagined. He scarcely knew who were his friends, nor where to look for aid.

At this juncture he was joined by one in whom he could place implicit confidence—it was his friend Troubridge, who, having been relieved in his blockade of Alexandria by Sir Sidney Smith, was once more placed under the orders of Nelson. Few officers in the navy possessed more sterling energy and honesty than Troubridge, and in firmness none excelled him. He was the one of all others suited for the peculiar state of affairs in the Mediterranean, and Nelson despatched him to harass the French at Naples. In the meanwhile, Nelson, though much against his inclination, remained at Palermo, the protector of the king.

Lord Nelson's orders to Captain Troubridge were dated 28th of March ; and the ships placed under his command were the *Minotaur, Zealous, Swiftsure, Seahorse, Perseus*, and *El Corso*. He was instructed to embark the Governor of Procida and 200 troops, and proceed to the Bay of Naples. He was directed to take possession of the island of Procida, as a refuge for the squadron, to reduce Ischia and Capri to subjection to the King of Naples, and to afford protection and assistance to the Ponza isles, which continued in their allegiance to his Sicilian majesty. These instructions were ably carried out, for on the 3rd of April Troubridge wrote,—" All the Ponza islands have the Neapolitan flag flying. Your lordship never beheld such loyalty ; the people are perfectly mad with joy, and asking for their beloved monarch. I have a villain, by name Francesco, on board, who commanded the castle of Ischia, formerly a Neapolitan officer, and of property in that island. The moment we took possession of the castle, the mob tore this vagabond's coat, with the tricoloured cape and cap of liberty button, to pieces ; and he had the impudence to put on his Sicilian majesty's regimentals again ; upon which, I tore his epaulets off, took his cockade out, and obliged him to throw them overboard. The mob entirely destroyed the tree of liberty, and tore the tricoloured flag into ten thousand pieces, so so that I have not been able to procure even a small remnant, to lay at the king's feet. I, however, send two pieces of the tree of liberty for *his majesty's fire.*" On the 13th of April Troubridge wrote :—" The whole of the islands are now in our possession. The governor, with 100 soldiers, is gone to settle the government of Capri, Vendutina, and Ponza. I enclose your lordship one of Caraccioli's letters, as head of the marine. This was intercepted at Capri."

While matters were thus progressing in the Bay of Naples, Sir Sidney Smith was actively engaged at the blockade of Alexandria. A misunderstanding occurred between Nelson and Sir Sydney. Sir Sydney Smith, having strangely construed his appointment as commodore into that of " commander-in-chief of the squadron in the Levant," the question was referred to Earl Spencer, to which his lordship replied :—" He [Sir Sidney Smith] was sent to serve in the Mediterranean fleet, and, of course, under your command, as well as that of every other officer senior to him, under Lord St. Vincent."

On the 25th of April, Troubridge writes :—" Oh, how I long to have a dash at the thieves! A person just from Naples tells me the Jacobins are pressing hard the French to remain. They begin to shake in their shoes. Those of the lower orders now speak freely. The rascally nobles, tired of standing as common sentinels, say, if they had known as much as they do now, they would have acted differently. The horrid treatment of the French has made all classes mad." May 1st, he wrote :—" Caraccioli, I am now satisfied, is a Jacobin. I enclose you one of his letters. He came in the gunboats to Castelamare himself, and spirited up the Jacobins." May 7th : —" Arbitello is sold, and I fear Longono will be the same." A desultory description of operations seems to have pervaded this portion of the blockade. On the 12th he wrote :—" Cockburn has just joined, and brings such famous news, that I am half mad with joy. The scoundrels will, and must, be annihilated."

It is rather important to remark in this place that Captain Troubridge, independent of the authority derived from Lord Nelson, was armed with instructions tantamount to a commission from the King of Sicily, by virtue of which he could place a Sicilian officer under arrest; and in the event of the officer's being tried by a court-martial of his own officers, and sentenced to death, he (Captain Troubridge) was authorised to carry the sentence into effect. In point of fact, the Sicilian authority of the commodore was very nearly, if not quite, equivalent to the British commission given by admiralty, and greater in some respects. On the 23rd of May, the singular present of the coffin, made from the shattered fragments of the main-mast of the *Orient*, was sent on board the *Vanguard*. The sailors construed it into a sign that a great battle was to ensue, and that Nelson had provided himself with a coffin for the occasion. Nelson had it set upright in his cabin, just behind the chair he usually occupied: but the terror of his servant, poor Tom Allen, was so great that he shuddered whenever he went near it, and he at last induced his master to have it sent below. Observing some of his captains eyeing it, Nelson said, "You may look if you like, but none of you shall have it." It was subsequently sent to his lordship's upholsterer in London, where it remained until after Nelson's death.

Nelson succeeded in restoring the King of Naples, but is by some held to have tarnished his fame by hanging Caraccioli, the Neapolitan admiral, who, however, certainly played him false, and betrayed the interests of his sovereign. Most biographers now agree that the execution may have been an error of judgment, but scarcely a stain on the honour of England's hero.

The French were expelled from the Neapolian territories, but Nelson perceived, when too late, that he had laboured in vain. While the dungeons of Naples were crowded with prisoners, frivolity and sensuality prevailed at the Court. Opportunities of cultivating the royalist feeling, which had so strongly manifested itself were disregarded and lost ; and, to crown all, Ferdinand resolved to proceed again to Palermo, whither Lord Nelson conveyed the Court on the 5th August. Commodore Troubridge remained at Naples. He was grieved at the folly of those for whom he had so gallantly fought, and chagrined that Nelson should have become so thoroughly engrossed by his royal friends. "I dread, my lord," he wrote, "all the feasting, etc., at Palermo. I am sure your health will be hurt. The king would be better employed digesting a good government. Everything gives way to their pleasures. The money spent at Palermo gives discontent here : fifty thousand people are unemployed, trade discouraged, and manufactures at a stand. It is the interest of many here to keep the king away ; they all dread reform ; their villanies are so deeply rooted, that, if some method is not taken to dig them out, this government cannot hold together. Out of twenty millions of ducats collected as revenue, only

thirteen millions reach the treasury." In a subsequent letter he wrote :—
" There are upwards of forty thousand families who have relations confined.
If some act of oblivion is not passed, there will be no end of persecution,
for the people of this country have no idea of anything but revenge, and to
gain a point would swear ten thousand false oaths. Constant efforts are
made to get a man taken up in order to rob him. The confiscated property
does not reach the king's treasury. All thieves ! It is selling for nothing.
His own people whom he employs are buying it up, and the vagabonds
pocket the whole."

But although dead to the sense of the iniquitous system of his government,
the king was alive to the obligations he was under to Nelson. In order to
give some substantial mark of his gratitude, the king conferred upon him
the dukedom of Bronte, in Sicily, accompanied by a domain, the estimated
value of which was £3,000 a-year. It, however, required much persuasion
to induce Nelson to accept the proffered honour ; and the only argument
which seemed to prevail over his scruples, was that used by Ferdinand himself. " Do you wish," said the king, " that your name alone should pass with
honour to posterity, and that I, Ferdinand Bourbon, should appear ungrate-
ful? " With the dukedom, which Nelson accepted conditionally upon the
permission of his own sovereign, a diamond-hilted sword was presented. It
had belonged to his father, Charles III. of Spain, and had been given to
Ferdinand on his accession to the throne of the Sicilies. The thought,
however, which gave Nelson most pleasure was that his name was familiar
to all classes throughout the world. The title, duke of Bronte (or thunder),
had also some charms for him ; but a present from a quarter wholly unexpected, added much to his self-gratulation. The Greek inhabitants of
Zante, though a small community, sent him a golden-headed sword and
truncheon, set round with as many diamonds as could be obtained in the
island. The grateful Greeks thanked him for having preserved that part of
the world from the horrors of anarchy, and prayed that his exploits might
accelerate the day, in which, amidst the glory and peace of thrones, the
miseries of the human race would cease. After landing the royal family at
Palermo, Nelson, with the exception of a cruise to Port Mahon, remained
at that port until the close of the year. He had, in fact, become the
guardian of the king.

During this time, in consequence of the absence of Lord Keith, Nelson was acting commander-in-chief, and, having completed the liberation of the Neapolitan states and the Roman territories, he pushed to the utmost of his power the reduction of Malta. The expulsion of the French from the Neapolitan territories, and the approach of the Russian army, under Suwarrow, had reduced them to the Roman states and the neighbourhood of Genoa, to which point Suwarrow's army was moving to their destruction. To free Rome from the presence of the French was Nelson's present object. He was aware that the Roman people were ready to welcome the enemies of the Fren h as friends, and thought that with about 1,200 troops to aid his fleet, he conld ensure the reduction of the forts of Civita Vecchia and St. Angelo. With this view, he applied to Sir James St. Clair Erskine, the temporary commandant of Minorca, but was unable to convince him that so small a force could act with success against regular fortresses. Deprived of this arm, Nelson ordered Troubridge, to whom he had left the command in the bay of Naples, to do the work with the fleet alone. Unable at that moment to leave his post, Troubridge sent Captain Hallowell to offer to the garrisons of Civita Vecchia and St. Angelo the same terms as those granted to Gaieta. The manner of the French officers at the interview, convinced Hallowell that they knew their own weakness, and feared the fleet. Upon this Troubridge acted ; a squadron under Captain Louis appeared off the Tiber, fresh negotiations were commenced, and in a very short time a capitulation for the entire Roman states was concluded. The English colours floated on St. Angelo, and Captain Louis acted as governor of the papal capital. Thus was fulfilled the prophecy of the Franciscan, that "Nelson would take Rome with his ships."

The capture of Malta had long formed a prominent object to the Mediterranean squadron. Five thousand French troops garrisoned its works, and rendered hopeless every attempt to reduce it, except by starvation. The Portuguese squadron, under the Marquis de Niza, assisted by such ships as could be spared from the other duties of the fleet, and a small ill-armed force of 1,500 peasants, aided by 500 English and Portuguese marines, endeavoured to prevent supplies from reaching the garrison from the land side. Captain Ball was governor and general, but though he was endeavouring his utmost to recover this island for the King of Sicily, he could obtain little or no help from that court. Had it not been for his energy and abilities, and the love which the natives bore towards him, Malta would not, to all appearance, have been captured for years. Men, money, and food were wanting. Nelson in vain endeavoured to obtain men from Minorca or from Russia. Money he now and then forced from the Sicilian court, and gathered food for his little army and the famishing islanders wherever he could.

After much persuasion, used with General Fox, who was now governor of Minorca, Colonel Graham was ordered to proceed to Malta, where he landed on the 10th of December, to assist in the siege ; but with means much too limited for the service required. Commodore Troubridge had previously received orders to proceed with the *Northumberland* and *Foudroyant* to co-operate with the colonel, and finding that money was wanting nobly supplied what he could from his own resources. " I procured 15,000 of my cobs— every farthing and every atom of me shall be devoted to the cause." Nelson, not to be outdone, declared he would sell Bronté, and the Emperor of Russia's box, and actually pledged the estate for £6,600, to answer any difficulty about paying the bills. But Nelson himself remained at Palermo. He, whose presence would have done so much, appeared enslaved by the frivolities he so much despised, although it may reasonably be supposed that he was influenced by higher motives. He was soon forcibly entreated by his rough though sincere friend Troubridge.

On the 1st January, 1800, he wrote:—" We are dying off fast for want. I learn that Sir William Hamilton says, Prince Luzzi refused corn some time ago, and Sir William does not think it worth while to make another application. If that be the case, I wish he commanded this distressing scene instead of me. I wish," he added, " I was at your lordship's elbow for an hour. All will be thrown upon you. I will parry the blow as much as in my power. I foresee much mischief brewing." To these and many like most urgent appeals Nelson responded to the best of his power. He begged almost on his knees for small supplies of money and corn, to keep the Maltese from starvation, and carry on the siege. The partial success his appeals met with would only have sufficed to prolong the misery of the famishing islanders, without permanently aiding the cause ; but Sir Thomas Troubridge and Captain Ball took a more decided course. Finding it vain to expect adequate supplies from Sicily, they took the law into their own hands, and despatched the *Stromboli*, Captain Broughton, to the port of Girgenti, with orders to purchase, or otherwise to seize and bring to Malta a fleet of vessels lying there corn-laden. The orders were obeyed, to the great relief and advantage of the shipowners, and the necessity of raising the siege was averted. The Neapolitan government complained to the British ambassador, and the latter to Nelson, who, no doubt, highly pleased at the decision of his friends, defended the act as one which had no alternative.

In the beginning of February, Nelson sailed from Palermo for Malta, and on his way was fortunate in capturing a French squadron. The following letter details the circumstances:—

"You, my dear friend," said he, writing to Lord Minto, "will rejoice to hear that it has been my extraordinary good fortune to capture the *Généreux,* 74, bearing the flag of Rear-Admiral Perrée, and a very large store-ship, with 2,000 troops, and provisions and stores for the relief of La Valette. I came off Malta with *my commander-in-chief,*—with Lord Keith; we parted company in bad weather the same day. Having information that such a squadron had sailed from Toulon, Lord K. remained off Malta; but with my knowledge of their track (rather, my knowledge of this country from seven years' experience), I went towards the coast of Barbary, where, three days afterwards, I fell in with the gentleman. Those ships which fell in with me after our separation from the commander-in-chief, attached themselves to my fortune. We took them, after a long chase, four miles only from Sicily, and a few leagues from Cape Passaro. Perrée was killed by a shot from the *Success* frigate, Captain Peard. His ship struck, when the *Foudroyant* fired only two shots. This, my dear lord, makes nineteen sail of the line and four admirals I have been present at the capture of this war. Ought I to trust Dame Fortune any more? Her daughter may step in and tear the mother from me. I have, in truth, serious thoughts of giving up the active service ; Greenwich Hospital seems a fit retreat for me, after being *evidently* thought unfit to command the Mediterranean."

Lord Keith had now returned, and resumed the command, much to Nelson's chagrin. In another letter he wrote:—"*We of the Nile* are not equal to Lord Keith in his estimation, and ought to think it an honour to serve under such a *clever* man." And, subsequently:—"As to my health, I believe I am almost finished. Many things, (some) of which you have felt in your time, contribute towards it. I am now on my route to my friends at Palermo. I shall there rest quiet for two weeks, and then judge by my feelings whether I am *able* to serve well, and with comfort to myself. It is said the combined fleet is coming this road, confiding it can escape as it did last year, but the pitcher never goes often to the well but it comes home broken at last."

One more Nile ship remained—the *Guillaume Tell*, which was at this time closely watched in the harbour of Valetta. After a daring attempt to escape, she surrendered to the *Foudroyant*, *Lion*, and *Penelope* frigate, and thus made a glorious finish to the Mediterranean fleet. Nelson was not present at her capture, and rejoiced that he had not taken a sprig from their laurels. "They are—and I glory in them," he wrote to Lord St. Vincent, "my children; they served in my school, and all of us caught our professional zeal and fire from the great and good Earl St. Vincent. What a pleasure, what a happiness, to have the Nile fleet all taken under my orders and regulations!" There were yet two frigates of that fleet in Valetta; one eventually got free, the other was captured. Such was the fate of the Nile fleet. Malta did not surrender until the 5th of September.

CHAPTER VI.

TRIUMPH AND RETURN HOME—SAILS FOR THE BALTIC—BATTLE OF COPENHAGEN.

1800—1801.

ON the 2nd June, Lord Nelson was appointed a knight grand cross of the order of St. Ferdinand and Merit of the Two Sicilies. On the 28th he shifted his flag from the *Foudroyant* to the *Alexander*, and on the 13th of July struck it, and left Leghorn on his way to England. He reached Florence on the 19th and Ancona on the 24th, where he embarked on board a Russian frigate for Trieste, and arrived there on the 9th of August. He remained a short time at Vienna, which he left on the 26th of September. He was obliged to adopt this route, as no ship could be spared from the fleet to take him direct home. He passed through Prague to Magdeburgh and Hamburgh, with his now inseparable friends, Sir William and Lady Hamilton. The most gratifying testimonials of esteem and admiration awaited him at every step. The Prince of Esterhazy entertained him in a style of Hungarian magnificence—a hundred grenadiers, each six feet in height, waiting at table. At Magdeburgh the master of the hotel gratified his friends and benefited himself by exhibiting the hero of the Nile for money, admitting the curious to peep at him through a small window.

A wine merchant at Hamburgh, who was above seventy years of age, requested to speak with Lady Hamilton, when he acquainted her ladyship that he had some Rhenish wine of the vintage of 1625, which had been in his own possession more than half a century. He had preserved it for some

93

extraordinary occasion, and that which had now presented itself was far beyond any he could have expected. He earnestly requested her assistance to
prevail upon his lordship to accept six dozen of this incomparable wine:
part of it would then have the honour to flow into the heart's blood of the
hero, and this thought would make him happy during the remainder of his
life. Nelson was delighted at the kindness of the old wine merchant, and
entering the room where he was, shook him affectionately by the hand, and
consented to receive six bottles of his wine provided he would promise to be
his guest at dinner next day. The invitation was joyfully accepted, and twelve
bottles were sent, six of which Nelson promised to put by to celebrate the half
dozen more victories he meant to gain. A German pastor, nearly eighty
years of age, travelled forty miles with the bible of his parish church to
request Nelson's autograph on the first leaf, for he considered him the saviour
of the Christian world.

The travellers landed at Yarmouth on the 6th of November, and this being
Nelson's first appearance in England since the Nile action, he was enthu-
siastically received. The populace assembled in crowds to greet him, and
taking the horses from his carriage, drew him to Wrestler's Inn, amid
tumultuous applause. The mayor and corporation lost no time in waiting
upon his lordship, and took the opportunity of presenting him with the
freedom of the town, which had some time previously been voted him, as an
acknowledgment of his eminent services. The infantry quartered in the town
paraded before the inn at which he lodged with their band, the soldiers fired
feux-de-joie, and firing of musketry and ordnance continued till midnight.

On the next day, the corporation in procession, together with the officers
of the navy residing near at hand, accompanied him to church with his
friends, and joined in a thanksgiving for his preservation. On leaving the
town a corps of cavalry met him, drew up, saluted, and then escorted the
carriage to the boundary of the county. On reaching Ipswich, similar
honours awaited him. In London, he was entertained on Lord Mayor's day
by the civic authorities, on which occasion his carriage was drawn by the
populace from Ludgate Hill to Guildhall. Here he received the thanks of
the court of common council and the golden-hilted sword, studded with
diamonds, which had been voted him immediately after the news of the
victory reached England. On the 20th he took his seat in the House of

Lords. Everywhere he was congratulated and treated as a successful hero, until he arrived at that spot in which is commonly centred the happiness of every good man—his home.

It was perhaps but too apparent that Lord Nelson's affection had been impaired by his last absence, and although we do not wish to cast any slur upon Lady Nelson, there seems good reason for believing that efforts were not made by her ladyship to regain by affectionate means the ascendancy she once possessed. As we cannot with safety pronounce Lord Nelson to be wholly wrong, nor his wife wholly right, we think it better to abstain from offering any further opinion of our own. It is enough to state that a final separation took place two months after Nelson's arrival in England. Previously to this, some difference had occured between his lordship and his step-son, Captain Nisbet.

One of Nelson's first acts on reaching England was to write an official letter to the secretary of the Admiralty announcing his return, and stating that as his health was perfectly re-established, he was ready for immediate employment. The Addington administration had not long been formed, and Earl St. Vincent was First Lord of the Admiralty. Nelson, on the 1st of January had been promoted to be vice-admiral, and he was not long in receiving orders to hoist his flag.

Denmark, Sweden, and Russia had formed a confederacy, with the view of compelling Great Britain to renounce her ancient right of search upon neutral property. Denmark acted under French dictation, and Sweden was governed by Denmark. Paul of Russia was instigated chiefly by caprice. The Danish fleet consisted of twenty-three sail of the line, and about thirty frigates and smaller vessels, but exclusive of guard and block ships, &c. Sweden had eighteen sail of the line, and a large fleet of frigates, galleys, and gunboats, numbering nearly one hundred. The Russian navy consisted of eighty-two sail of the line, forty-seven of which were at Cronstadt, Revel, St. Petersburgh, and Archangel; but they were badly officered and manned. A coalition so formidable, especially when considered with reference to the growing power of the French republic, demanded active operations. The chief command of the fleet in the Baltic was at this time vested in Admiral Sir Hyde Parker, and who being already thus employed, could not with propriety be displaced.

On the 17th of January, Lord Nelson hoisted his vice-admiral's flag on board the *San Josef*, at Plymouth ; on the 21st he received the freedom of the city of Exeter, and on the 24th was admitted a freeman of the borough of Plymouth. On the 12th of February he shifted his flag to the *Saint George*, and on the 17th was ordered to place himself under the orders of Sir Hyde Parker. On the 21st the *Saint George* arrived at Spithead. According to a statement contained in a narrative of the events which took place before and at the battle of Copenhagen, written by the Honourable Colonel Stewart, who was in command of the troops, the *Saint George*, while at Portsmouth, required considerable repairs. On the 27th of February the troops, consisting of 760 rank and file, proceeded to Southsea Common, waiting orders. " Lord Nelson," says the narrator, "arrived from London about 10h. A.M. He sent for me immediately on his arrival. On first acquaintance I witnessed the activity of his character : he said that not a moment was to be lost in embarking the troops, for he intended to sail next tide. Lord Nelson in three hours after left the sally-port for the *Saint George*. The ship was commanded by his old friend Captain Hardy, and was undergoing considerable repairs at Spithead—the caulkers and painters were detained on board, and we proceeded with them to St. Helens. The wind became fair in the course of the night, and we got under way at daylight on the 28th. Nothing particular occurred till our arrival in the Downs : the seine was frequently hauled by Lord Nelson's directions, and the eagerness and vivacity which he showed upon the occasion, to the great delight of the seamen, early pointed out to me the natural liveliness of his character, even in trivial matters.

" Another trait may be worthy of remark as illustrative of much *naïveté*. His lordship was rather too apt to interfere in the working of the ship, and not always with the best success or judgment. The wind, when off Dunge-ness, was scant, and it was necessary to put the ship about. Lord Nelson would give the orders, and he, in consequence, caused her to miss stays. Upon this he said, rather peevishly, to the master, or officer of the watch (I forget which), 'Well, now, see what *we* have done. Well, sir, what do you mean to do now?' The officer saying, with hesitation, 'I don't exactly know, my lord, I fear she won't do,' Lord Nelson turned sharply towards the cabin, and replied, 'Well, I am sure, if you don't know what to do with her, no more do I either.' He went in, leaving the officer to work the ship as he liked. He visited on shore at Deal his old friend Admiral Lutwidge. We sailed on the succeeding morning, and entered Yarmouth Roads on the 6th or 7th of March. The *Saint George* was the first three-decker which had so done."

The British Cabinet, hoping to settle the disputed points by negotiation, ordered Mr. Nicholas Vansittart (afterwards Lord Bexley) to embark for that purpose. Nelson felt somewhat surprised at the apparent want of deference observed towards him by the admiral. Having heard of some of the plans, he thus expressed himself in a letter to Mr. Davison :—" All I have gathered of our first plans I disapprove of most exceedingly : honour may arise from them, good cannot. I hear we are likely to anchor outside Cronenburg Castle, instead of at Copenhagen—which would give weight to our negotiation. A Danish minister would think twice before he would put his name to war with England, when the next moment he would probably see his master's fleet in flames, and his capital in ruins ; but ' out of sight out of mind' is an old saying. The Dane should see our flag waving every moment he lifted up his head." On reaching the Scaw Mr. Vansittart left the fleet, and proceeded to Copenhagen in the *Blanche* frigate with a flag of truce. Doubtless Lord Nelson's plan would have been infinitely more effective. No preparations had at that time been made for the defence of the place ; and hundreds of lives of brave men would have been saved by prompt measures. Nelson's opinion was, that a negotiation always produced a better effect when supported by the battery of a man-of-war.

On the 23rd he was invited to a long conference with Sir Hyde Parker, and on the 24th addressed the admiral a most masterly letter. The following are extracts :—" The more I have reflected the more I am confirmed in opinion that not a moment should be lost in attacking the enemy: the only consideration in my mind is, how to get at them with the least risk to our ships. By Mr. Vansittart's account, the Danes have taken every means in their power to prevent our getting to Copenhagen by the passage of the Sound ; Cronenburg has been strengthened ; the Crown Islands fortified, on the outermost of which are twenty guns, pointing mostly down. wards, and only 800 yards from very formidable batteries placed under the citadel, supported by five sail of the line, seven floating batteries of fifty

4

guns each, besides small craft, gun-boats, etc., etc. ; and that the Revel
squadron of twelve or fourteen sail of the line is soon expected, as also five
sail of Swedes. Therefore, here you are with almost the safety—certainly
the honour—of England more entrusted to you than ever yet fell to the lot
of any British officer. On your decision depends whether our country shall
be degraded in the eyes of Europe, or whether she shall rear her head
higher than ever; again do I repeat, never did our country depend so much
on the success of any fleet as on this." After describing most graphically
the modes of action open for adoption, he thus concludes his letter :—
"Supposing us through the Belt, with the wind first westerly, would it not
be possible to either go with the fleet, or detach ten ships of two or three
decks, with one bomb, and two fire ships, to Revel, to destroy the Russian
squadron at that place? I do not see the great risk of such a detachment,
and with the remainder to attempt the business at Copenhagen. The
measure may be thought bold, but I am of opinion the boldest measures
are the safest ; and our country demands a most vigorous exertion of her
force directed with judgment. In supporting you, my dear Sir Hyde,
through the arduous and important task you have undertaken, no exertion
of head or heart shall be wanting from me."

The following succinct account of the action, taken from the pages of a
popular work on naval battles, shows as briefly as is consistent with the
subject the principal features of the action.

"After some further delay and useless negotiation, the British fleet got
under way at 6h. A.M. on the 30th of March, and with a fine breeze at
north-north-west formed in line ahead, and proceeded up the Sound ; the
van division commanded by Vice-Admiral Lord Nelson, the centre by
Admiral Sir Hyde Parker, and the rear by Rear-Admiral Thomas Graves.
At 7h. A.M. the batteries at Elsineur opened fire upon the *Monarch*, but
without doing any damage ; and only a few ships fired in return, except the
bomb-vessels, which threw more than 200 shells into Cronenburg and
Helsingen, doing much execution. The only casualty in the British fleet
was occasioned by the bursting of a 24-pounder on board the *Isis*, by which
accident seven men were killed and wounded. The fleet continued its
course, keeping within a mile of the Swedish shore, on which only eight

guns were mounted, and thus avoided the fire of 100 pieces of cannon mounted in the castle of Cronenburg.

"About noon, the fleet anchored above the island of Huën, and fifteen miles below Copenhagen. The three admirals, with Captain Domett, Colonel Stewart, and others, then proceeded in the *Lark* lugger to reconnoitre the defences of the enemy ; and in the evening a council of war was held on board the *London*, at which Lord Nelson offered to conduct an attack with ten sail of the line and all the smaller vessels. The proposal was accepted by Sir Hyde Parker, who added two ships of the line to the force demanded.

"The Danes, in order to render the approach—at times exceedingly intricate—more difficult, had removed the buoys, and Lord Nelson, accompanied by Captain James Brisbane, proceeded in his boat to rebuoy the outer channel.

"On the morning of the 1st of April, the fleet weighed, and anchored again about six miles from Copenhagen, off the north-western extremity of the middle ground, which shoal extends along the whole sea front of the city, with the King's Channel inside, about three-quarters of a mile in width, in which channel the Danish block ships, radeaus, prames, and gun-vessels, were moored. In the forenoon, Lord Nelson embarked on board the *Amazon*, and again reconnoitred the Danish force ; and soon after his return, at 1h. P.M., ordered the signal to weigh to be hoisted on board the *Elephant*. This signal was received by loud cheers from the different ships of the fleet ; and in a very short time the Vice-Admiral's squadron, amounting in all to thirty-six sail, were under way, and formed in two divisions, with a light but favourable air of wind, leaving Sir Hyde Parker at anchor with eight sail of the line.

"The *Amazon* leading, the British squadron passed along the edge of the middle ground, until it had reached the southern extremity, and at about 8h. P.M. anchored ; the headmost ship of the British being then about two miles from the southernmost ship of the Danish line. During the night, Captain Hardy was employed in sounding the channel, and passed completely round one of the enemy's floating batteries unperceived ; and about 11h. P.M. returned to the *Elephant*, and reported the depth of water close up to the Danish fleet.

"At the northern extremity of their line, which extended above a mile and a-half, were the two Trekroner batteries formed on piles ; one mounting thirty long 24-pounders, and the other thirty-eight long 36-pounders, with furnaces for heating shot. These batteries were each commanded by two two-decked block ships, the *Mars* and *Elephanten*, not included in the foregoing list. A chain was thrown across the entrance to the inner harbour (as it may be termed, to distinguish it from the outer roadstead in which the flotilla was moored), which was also protected by the crown batteries, and in addition, by the 74-gun ships *Trekroner* and *Dannemark*, a 40-gun frigate, two brigs, and some armed boats, which latter were provided with furnaces for heating shot. On the island of Amag, to the southward of the line, were several gun and mortar batteries. The whole Danish force was under the command of Commodore Olfert Fischer, who had his broad pennant flying on board the 62-gun ship *Dannebrog*.

" At 8h. A.M., on the 22nd of April, the signal was made for the captains of the several ships, to each of whom Lord Nelson assigned his several station. The intention was, that all the ships of the line should take their places abreast of the enemy's ships, anchoring by the stern ; while the frigates were to attack the ships off the harbour's mouth, and to rake the southern extremity of the Danish line. It was also intended that the 49th regiment, under Colonel Stewart, and 500 seamen, under Captain Fremantle, should storm the largest of the crown batteries. These plans, however, were many of them frustrated by the accidents which happened. At 9h. 30m. (wind south-east), the pilots assembled on board the *Elephant*, when their want of knowledge and indecision became evident, and it would have been well had the opinion of Captain Hardy been taken. However, the signal was made to weigh. The *Edgar* led, and the *Agamemnon* was to have followed her ; but the wind being scant, and a strong tide running, the latter found it impossible to get round the southern end of the shoal, and after two or three attempts was compelled to anchor. The *Polyphemus* then became the second ship, followed by the *Isis*. The *Bellona*, owing to the ignorance of her pilot—although she had rounded the point—got ashore on the middle ground, about 450 yards from the rear of the Danish line, where, however, she was within reach of the enemy's shot. The *Russell* following her leader very closely, also grounded with her jib-boom almost over the *Bellona's* taffrail.

" The *Elephant*, bearing Lord Nelson's flag, was the next ship, but in opposition to the pilots, on observing the accident to two of his ships, Lord Nelson ordered the *Elephant's* helm to be put a-starboard, and she passed to the westward, and on the larboard side of the *Bellona*. The remaining ships following the same course, succeeded in getting into action. At 10h. the firing commenced; but the ships principally engaged for the first half-hour were the *Polyphemus*, *Isis*, *Edgar*, *Monarch*, and *Ardent*. At 11h. 30m. the *Glatton*, *Elephant*, *Ganges*, and *Defiance*, as well as several of the smaller vessels, had reached their several stations; and the *Désirée*, by directing a raking fire at the *Provesteen*, drew part of her attention from the *Isis*, which latter ship, however, suffered very severely. The strong tide prevented the *Jamaica* and the gun-vessels from getting near enough to take part in the action, nor did the bombs perform much service. The grounding of the *Bellona* and *Russell*, and the absence of the *Agamemnon*, occasioned some of the British ships to have more than one opponent. The *Amazon* suffered considerably, Captain Riou having anchored her, with three other frigates and the sloops, abreast of the Trekroner batteries.

" The engagement had continued three hours, and no ship in the Danish line had ceased firing. On the other hand, signals of distress were flying on board the *Russell* and *Bellona*, and the *Agamemnon* had hoisted that of inability. The *Veteran*, *Defence*, and *Ramillies* had been detached to re-inforce Lord Nelson; but their progress was so slow, that Sir Hyde Parker was induced to order the signal to be made to discontinue the action.

" Lord Nelson was at this time," writes Colonel Stewart, " as he had been during the whole action, walking the starboard side of the quarter deck—sometimes much animated, and at others heroically fine in his observations. A shot through the mainmast knocked a few splinters about us. He observed to me, with a smile, ' It is warm work, and this day may be the last to any of us at a moment;' and then, stopping short at the gangway, he used an expression never to be erased from my memory, and said with emotion, ' but mark you, I would not be elsewhere for thousands!' When the signal No. 39 was made, the signal-lieutenant reported it to him. He continued his walk, and did not appear to take notice of it. The lieutenant, meeting his lordship at the next turn, asked whether he should repeat it? Lord Nelson answered, ' No; acknowledge it.' On the officer returning to the poop, his lordship called after him, ' Is No. 16 (for close action) still hoisted?' The lieutenant answered in the affirmative. Lord Nelson said, ' Mind you keep it so.' He now walked the deck considerably agitated—which was also known by his moving the stump of his right arm. After a turn or two, he said to me in a quick manner, ' Do you know what's shown on board the Commander-in-chief, No. 39?' On asking him what it meant, he answered, ' Why, to leave off action ! Leave off action,' he repeated—and then added, with a shrug, a very strong expletive. He then observed, I believe to Captain Foley, ' You know, Foley, I have only one eye—I have a right to be blind sometimes ;' and then, with an archness peculiar to his character, putting the glass to his blind eye, he exclaimed, ' I really do not see the signal.' This remarkable signal was therefore only acknowledged on board the *Elephant*, not repeated. Admiral Graves did the latter, not being able to distinguish the *Elephant's* conduct ; and, either by a fortunate accident, or intentionally, No. 16 was not hauled down."

It has been confidently argued by Southey, and admitted by Mr. James, that Sir Hyde Parker, in making this signal, left it to Nelson to do as he pleased, and that it was only tantamount to a permission to retire, if the enemy was found too strong. This supposition, however, cannot be received by professional men. The signal book was before him, and Sir Hyde could have telegraphed his " permission " in a more intelligible way ; but the signal of recall was peremptory, and Nelson disobeyed it at the peril of his commission. Success took it out of Sir Hyde Parker's power to vindicate the rules of the service, had he been (which we do not think he was) inclined to do so ; but it is extremely questionable if failure would have been an equally good palliative of disobedience.

The frigates, in obedience to the signal, hauled off from the Crown batteries ; and the *Amazon* became exposed to their heavy fire, by which Captain Riou was cut in two, and many others added to the slain. At 1h. 30m. P.M., the firing of the Danes slackened, and before 2h. it had ceased in all the ships astern of the *Zealand* ; but none of the vessels would allow the British to take possession, and as the boats approached for that purpose, they were fired at by the Danes, continually reinforced from the shore. This extraordinary mode of warfare irritated Lord Nelson, who was almost induced to order the fire-ships in to burn the surrendered vessels ; but he first determined to try the effect of negotiation, by addressing a letter to the Crown Prince of Denmark.

His lordship's letter ran thus :—"Vice-Admiral Lord Nelson has been commanded to spare Denmark, when no longer resisting. The line of defence which covered her shores has struck to the British flag ; but if the firing is continued on the part of Denmark, he must set on fire all the prizes he has taken, without having the power of saving the men who have so nobly defended them. The brave Danes are the brothers, and should never be the enemies, of England." A wafer was handed to his lordship for the letter ; but with that coolness and ability which ever distinguished him, he remarked that this was no time to appear hurried and informal, and ordered a candle to be brought from the cockpit. His lordship sealed the letter with wax, affixing a larger impression than usual. Sir Frederick Thesiger (a young commander, acting as one of Lord Nelson's *aides-de-camp*) was then despatched on shore with the letter and a flag of truce, and meeting the Crown Prince at the sally port, delivered the letter.

In the meantime, the cannonade was continued by the *Defiance, Monarch*, and *Ganges*, which, in a short time, silenced the *Indusforethen, Holstein*, and the ships next them in the Danish line. The approach of the *Defence, Ramillies*, and *Veteran*, also rendered the case of the Danes hopeless. The great Crown battery, however, having been reinforced by 1,500 men, continued firing ; and it was deemed advisable to withdraw the ships from before it, while the wind continued fair. Preparations were making for carrying this into effect, when the Danish adjutant-general, Lindholm, appeared bearing a flag of truce, upon which the action, which had raged incessantly for four hours, totally ceased. The message from the Crown Prince was to enquire the precise object of Lord Nelson's note, when the latter replied, in writing, that humanity was his object ; that he consented to stay hostilities ; that the wounded Danes should be taken on shore ; that he would take his prisoners out of the vessels, and burn or carry off the prizes, as he thought fit ; and concluded by expressing a hope that the victory he had gained would lead to a reconciliation between the two countries. This answer being returned, the final adjustment of the terms was referred to the commander-in-chief. "During the interval, the British ships were moved from their stations in the line, in doing which several grounded ; the *Elephant* and *Defiance*, in particular, remained fast for many hours, about a mile from the Trekroner battery."

The table shows the loss sustained by the ships of the British squadron, in the order in which they entered the action :—

Ships.	Killed.	Wounded.	Ships.	Killed.	Wounded.
Désirée	—	4	Brought forward	139	420
Russell	—	6	*Ganges*	7	1
Bellona	11	72	*Monarch*	56	164
Polyphemus	6	25	*Defiance*	24	51
Isis	33	88	*Amazon*	14	23
Edgar	31	111	*Blanche*	7	9
Ardent	30	64	*Alcmène*	5	19
Glatton	18	37	*Dart*	3	1
Elephant	10	13			
			Total.........	255	688
Carried forward	139	420			

Of those numbered amongst the wounded a large proportion were dangerously, and many mortally ; and Mr. James estimates that on the whole the British loss may be thus stated — killed and mortally wounded, 350 ; recoverably and slightly, 850. It is quite evident that so heavy a loss could only have resulted from cool and steady firing on the part of the Danes, who did not aim at dismasting the British ships ; indeed only one ship (the *Glatton*) lost a topmast. Several ships had guns disabled. The loss on board the Danish ships, according to the very lowest estimate, amounted to between 1,600 and 1,800 men killed and wounded, and probably far exceeded the highest of these numbers.

The letter of Lord Nelson to the commander-in-chief briefly recapitulated the events of the day :—

" *Elephant*, 3rd April.

"In obedience to your directions to report the proceedings of the squadron named in the margin, which you did me the honour to place under my command, I beg leave to inform you, that having, by the assistance of that able officer, Captain Riou, and the unremitting exertions of Captain Brisbane, and the masters of the *Amazon* and *Cruiser* in particular, buoyed the channel of the Outer deep and the position of the Middle Ground, the squadron passed in safety, and anchored off Draco the evening of the first ; and that yesterday morning I made the signal for the squadron to weigh and engage the Danish line, consisting of six sail of the line, eleven floating batteries, mounting from twenty-six 24-pounders to eighteen 18-pounders, and one bomb-ship, besides schooner gun-vessels. These were supported by the Crown islands, mounting eighty-eight cannon, and four sail of the line moored in the harbour's mouth, and some batteries on the island of Amak. The bomb-shells and schooner made their escape, the other seventeen sail are sunk, burnt, or taken, being the whole of the Danish line to the southward of the Crown Islands, after a battle of four hours.

" From the very intricate navigation, the *Bellona* and *Russell* unfortunately grounded ; but although not in the situation assigned them, yet so placed as to be of great service. The *Agamemnon* could not weather the shoal of the Middle, and was obliged to anchor ; but not the smallest blame can be attached to Captain Fancourt ; it was an event to which all the ships were liable. These accidents prevented the extension of our line by the three ships before mentioned, who would, I am confident, have silenced the Crown islands, the two other ships in the harbour's mouth, and prevented the heavy loss in the *Defiance* and *Monarch*, and which, unhappily, threw the gallant and good Captain Riou (to whom I had given the command of the frigates and sloops named in the margin, to assist in the attack of the ships at the harbour's mouth) under a heavy fire ; the consequence has been the death of Captain Riou and many brave officers and men in the frigates and sloops. The bombs took their stations abreast of the *Elephant*, and threw some shells into the arsenal. Captain Rose, who volunteered his services to direct the gun-brigs, did everything that was possible to get them forward, but the current was too strong for them to be of service during the action ; but not the less merit is due to Captain Rose—and I believe all the officers and crews of the gun-brigs—for their exertions. The boats of those ships of the fleet that were not ordered on the attack afforded us every assistance, and the officers and men who were in them merited my

warmest approbation.   The *Désirée* took her station in raking the southern·
most Danish ship of the line, and performed the greatest service.

 "The action began at five minutes past ten.   The van, led by Captain
George Murray, of the *Edgar*, was as well followed up by every captain,
officer, and man in the squadron.   It is my duty to state to you the high
and distinguished merit and gallantry of Rear-Admiral Graves.   To Captain
Foley, who permitted me the honour of hoisting my flag in the *Elephant*, I
feel under the greatest obligations ; his advice was necessary on many
important occasions during the battle.   I beg leave to express how much I
feel indebted to every captain, officer, and man, for their zeal and distin·
guished bravery on this occasion.   The honourable Colonel Stewart did me
the favour to be on board the *Elephant*, and himself, with every other officer
and soldier under his orders, shared with pleasure the toils and dangers of
the day.   The loss in such a battle has necessarily been very heavy.   Among
many other brave officers and men who were killed, I have with sorrow to
place the name of Captain Mosse, of the *Monarch*, who has left a wife and
six children to lament his loss ; and among the wounded, that of Captain
Sir Thomas B. Thompson, of the *Bellona*."

Nelson's services had, however, been of too brilliant and successful a
character to incur even a momentary censure, and if any such idea was
seriously entertained by him, it was immediately removed by his reception
on board the *London*, whither he was repairing.   Sir Hyde Parker, what·
ever he might have felt, expressed to Nelson his complete satisfaction and
grateful acknowledgments.   It was agreed that there should be a suspension
of hostilities for twenty-four hours—that the prizes should be peacefully
yielded up by the Danes, and the wounded Danes sent on shore.   This
latter, though apparently a concession, was, in fact, imperative, for the
Danes had provided no surgeons on board their ships, in consequence of
which the mutilated and wounded sufferers were lying upon the decks of
"he prizes bleeding to death!

All night the boats of the fleet were actively employed bringing out the
Danes, and getting the grounded ships afloat.   Nelson had, meanwhile,
gone on board the *Saint George* to sleep, but at daybreak on the morning
of the 3rd, returned in his gig to the *Elephant*, which, to his satisfaction, he
found again afloat.   After partaking of a hasty breakfast, he turned his

attention to the prizes. The 74-gun ship *Zealand*, which was the last to surrender, had drifted on a shoal under the *Trekroner*, and, trusting to the protection that battery could afford, the commander declined to yield her up as a prize. Having ordered a brig and three launches to approach the *Zealand*, Nelson proceeded on board the *Hagen*, one of the Danish radeaus, intending to communicate with Commodore Fischer, whose broad pennant was flying on board the *Dannebrog*. The *Hagen* was in command of an old West Indian acquaintance—Lieutenant Müller. Nelson, uninvited, went on board, and acted with such ability and politeness towards his old friend and the officers assembled, that he not only gained his point with respect to the *Zealand*, but acquired their good will and admiration. The *Zealand* was soon afterwards towed off the bank by her captors, to the extreme mortification of the Danes—who were still unwilling to allow themselves conquered. It was resolved that Nelson should wait on the Crown Prince on the following day.

On the afternoon of the 4th, his lordship, attended by Captains Fremantle and Hardy, accordingly landed, and was received with every mark of attention. The feelings of the populace were of a mingled kind—admiration, curiosity, grief, and displeasure. A strong guard protected Nelson from any unpleasant demonstration, while his boldness in venturing among his late enemies so soon after the great calamity he had occasioned, inspired them with a sort of awe. Never before had a shot been fired upon the inhabitants of Copenhagen in anger, and now their town had been in great part involved in their fleet's destruction. It must have appeared the height of rashness; but Nelson knew no consideration paramount to his duty to his country, and which he thought demanded his presence on shore. So careless was he of his personal safety, that, although a carriage had been provided to convey him to the palace of the crown prince, he declined the offer. After dining with his royal highness, he opened the subject of the negotiation, but it took several days to settle the various points in dispute. In the meanwhile, the British were actively employed removing and destroying the prizes, and in refitting the ships, so as to be ready to renew the action.

On the 9th Lord Nelson went on shore again, accompanied by General Lindholm, Colonel Stewart, Captain Edward Thornborough Parker, the

Reverend Mr. Scott, his lordship's chaplain, &c. He was escorted to the palace, but was no longer the object of suppressed disapprobation to the crowd. The commissioners appointed to arrange the business immediately entered on their task. Anticipation of the displeasure of Russia was a great point to be overcome with the Danes. The seventh article, proposing an armistice of sixteen weeks, was objected to on that score, upon which Nelson, with more bluntness than diplomacy, stated that his reason for requiring so long a term, in order that he might have time to act against the Russian fleet before returning to them. The point not being acceded to on either side, one of the Danish commissioners hinted at the renewal of hostilities as the alternative. Nelson, who understood French sufficiently well to comprehend the meaning of the observation, turned to one of his friends, and said, with warmth, " Renew hostilities ! Tell him we are ready at a moment ; ready to bombard this very night." The commissioner apologised, and the conference went on more amicably. The meeting broke up at two o'clock. The duration of the armistice could not, however, be adjusted, and the point was referred to the Crown Prince.

A levee was consequently held in one of the state rooms, the whole of which were without furniture, from the apprehension of a bombardment. They then proceeded to a grand dinner, the prince leading the way. Nelson, leaning on the arm of a friend, whispered,—" Though I have only one eye, I see all this will burn very well ;"—the bombardment was evidently uppermost in his mind. Nelson sat at the prince's right hand, and much cordiality prevailed throughout the entertainment. The disputed article was at length arranged by substituting " fourteen " for sixteen weeks.

Nelson on this occasion bore noble testimony to the heroic and protracted defence of the Danes. He eulogised their conduct in the highest terms, and declared to the prince that this had been the most tremendous action in which he had ever been engaged. He particularly named a gallant youth, Lieutenant Villenoes, who commanded a floating battery, or, more properly speaking, raft ; for it was loosely constructed of a number of spars bolted together, and overlaid with a platform upon which to work the guns. It was simply a square breastwork full of port-holes, and without masts, and was named Grenier's float. The skill and effect with which the raft was managed in the heat of the action attracted the attention of Lord Nelson.

He particularly requested to be introduced to the officer—a stripling of seventeen ; and this being complied with, he greeted him with much warmth, and, turning to the prince, said, "He ought to be made an admiral." The prince replied, " If I were to make all my brave officers admirals, I should have no lieutenants left."

Sir Hyde Parker, considering that it would cost more to fit the prizes for sea than they were worth, ordered them, with the exception of the *Holstein*, sixty-four, to be burnt. The *Zealand*, the finest of the ships, was in tolerably good condition, and her destruction gave much dissatisfaction to the gallant captors.

The honours awaiting Nelson and his daring band, were wholly incommensurate with the service performed. No gold medals were granted, and the City of London omitted to pay the usual tribute of its admiration—a fact of which Nelson did not forget to remind the Lord Mayor on a subsequent occasion. Lord Nelson was created a viscount, the commanders were posted, and senior lieutenants of the ships engaged made commanders. Rear-admiral Graves was made a Knight of the Bath, the investiture taking place on board the St. George. The thanks of both Houses of Parliament were voted on the 16th of April. In the House of Lords, Earl St. Vincent declared that the conduct of the officers engaged in the expedition had far surpassed anything that was to be found in the glorious annals of the British navy. The Duke of Clarence highly complimented Lord Nelson on his skill and intrepidity, which fortune seemed to back in every enterprise in which he was engaged. Lord Hood said he could not content himself with giving a silent vote ; because he had been personally convinced, while he had the honour of having those two illustrious officers (Lord Nelson and Sir Hyde Parker) serving under him, that it was impossible there could be two more courageous and able commanders, or who were more zealous in their country's cause. The tribute paid in the House of Commons was not less flattering. Mr. Addington, who moved the thanks of the house, declared that " no action had taken place in the course of the war which had contributed more to sustain the character, or to add to the lustre of the British arms. Great as was the courage and skill which had formerly been displayed by this illustrious commander at Aboukir, it was no greater than that which had been exhibited in the attack upon the fleet moored for the

defence of Copenhagen. But this was not all. After the line of defence
was destroyed, and while a tremendous fire was still continued, Lord
Nelson retired to his cabin, and addressed a letter to the Prince Royal of
Denmark. He then asked that a flag of truce might be permitted to land,
adding, at the same time, that if this was denied, he must be obliged to
demolish the floating batteries that were in his power ; and that in such
case, he could not answer for the lives of the brave men by whom they had
been defended. To the answer which required to know the motive of such
a measure, his reply was—that his only motive was humanity ; that his
wish was to prevent the farther effusion of blood ; and that no victory which
he could possibly gain would afford him so much pleasure as would result
from his being the instrument of restoring the amicable intercourse which
had so long existed between his sovereign and the government of Denmark.
The manner in which his lordship had spoken of Admiral Graves, Colonel
Stewart, and the rest of the officers who had co-operated with him, showed
the kindness of his nature, and the gallantry of his spirit."

On the 9th of April, Nelson wrote to Earl St. Vincent : "Just returned
from getting the armistice ratified. I am tired to death. None but those
on the spot can tell what I have gone through, and do suffer. I make no
scruple in saying that I would have been at Revel fourteen days ago ; that
without this armistice the fleet could never have gone but by order from the
Admiralty, and with it I dare say we shall not go this week. I wanted Sir
Hyde to let me at least go and cruise off Carlscrona to prevent the Revel
ships from getting in. I said I would not go to Revel to take any of those
laurels which I was sure he would reap there. Think for me, my dear lord,
and if I have deserved well, let me retire ; if ill, for heaven's sake supersede
me—for I cannot exist in this state." About the same time, or rather
before, he evinced his care and anxiety for the interests of his officers and
men. "Whether Sir Hyde Parker may mention the subject to you I know
not, for he is rich and does not want it. Nor is it, you will believe me,
from any desire I possess to get a few hundred pounds that actuates me in
addressing this letter to you ; but justice to the brave officers and men who
fought on that day. It is true our opponents were in hulks and floats, only
adapted for the position they were placed in, but that made our battle so
much the harder, and victory so much the more difficult to obtain. I think

the king should send a gracious message to the House of Commons for a gift to this fleet—for what must be the natural feelings of the officers and men belonging to it, to see their rich commander-in-chief burn all the fruits of their victory, which if fitted up and sent to England, as many of them might have been, would have sold for a good round sum."

In consequence of the exaggerated statements in Commodore Fischer's letter, and some other mis-statements, Lord Nelson addressed a letter to General Lindholm, dated April 22nd, 1801. In it he says,—"I am ready to admit that many of the Danish officers and men behaved as well as men could do, and deserved not to be abandoned by their commander. I am justified in saying this from Commodore Fischer's own declaration. In his letter he states that, after he quitted the *Dannebrog*, she long contested the battle. If so, more shame for him to quit so many brave fellows. *Here* was no manœuvring ; it was downright fighting, and it was his duty to have shown an example of firmness becoming the high trust reposed in him. He went in such a hurry, if he went before she struck (which but from his own declaration I can hardly believe), that he forgot to take his broad pennant with him ; for both pennant and ensign were struck together, and it is from this circumstance that I claimed the commodore as a prisoner of war. He then went, as he said, on board the *Holstein*, the brave captain of which did not want him, where he did not hoist his pennant. From this ship he went on shore either before or after she struck, or he would have been again a prisoner. As to his nonsense about victory, his royal highness will not much credit him. I sunk, burnt, captured, or drove into the harbour the whole line of defence to the southward of the Crown Islands.

"He says he is told that two British ships struck. Why did he not take possession of them? The reason is clear—that he did not believe it. He must have known the falsity of the report, and that no fresh British ships did come near the ships engaged. He states that the ship in which I had the honour to hoist my flag fired latterly only single guns. It is true—for steady and cool were my brave fellows, and I did not wish to throw away a single shot. He seems to exult that I sent on shore a flag of truce. Men of his description, if they are ever victorious, know not the feeling of humanity. You know, and his royal highness knows, that the guns fired from the shore could only fire through the Danish ships which had surrendered, and that if I fired at the shore it could only be in the same manner. God forbid I should destroy a non-resisting Dane! When they became my prisoners, I became their protector. Humanity alone could have been my object, but Mr. Fischer's carcase was safe, and he regarded not the sacred call of humanity. His royal highness thought as I did. It has brought about an armistice, which, I pray the Almighty, may bring about a happy reconciliation between the two kingdoms."

General Lindholm replied to Nelson's comments upon the Danish commodore's letter, with much good taste. He vindicated his countryman in some points, and excused him upon others. He repudiated the idea of claiming as a victory that which he knew well was a defeat—although far from being an inglorious one. "As to your lordship's motive for sending a flag of truce," said the general, "it can never be misconstrued; and your subsequent conduct has sufficiently shown that humanity is always the companion of true valour. You have done more—you have shown yourself a friend to the re-establishment of peace and good harmony between this country and Great Britain. It is, therefore, with the sincerest esteem, I shall always feel myself attached to your lordship."

On the 12th of April, the fleet under Sir Hyde Parker sailed from Copenhagen, leaving the *St. George* and one or two frigates in the roads. To the surprise of the Danes and the Swedes, the fleet took the passage between the islands of Amak and Saltholm, with the intention of attacking the Russian fleet at Revel. Several ships grounded, owing to the shoalness of the navigation. But hearing that the Swedish squadron of nine sail of the line were at sea, Sir Hyde Parker directed his course to the northern end of Bornholm. The Swedes, however, had entered Carlscrona. Nelson, although he had expressed his willingness to relinquish his share of laurels to Sir Hyde Parker, was, in the meanwhile, upon thorns. He hasted to complete the work of his ship, and on the 18th, was prepared to follow the fleet. The *St. George*, however, drew too much water to take the passage the fleet had made, with her guns on board. Nelson, therefore, had these trans-shipped on board an American vessel, but a contrary wind still delayed him.

While thus detained, information reached him that there was a probability of a meeting between the British and Swedish fleets. A distance of at least one hundred and fifty miles was interposed between them, but a greater would not have kept Nelson from attempting a junction. He immediately ordered a six-oared cutter to be manned. A cold night was setting in ; but he determined to proceed. The master of the Bellona, Mr. Briarly, who accompanied him, has thus narrated what passed on the occasion :—

"Without even waiting for a boat-cloak (although you may suppose the weather pretty sharp here at this season of the year, and having to row about twenty-four miles, with the wind and current against him), he jumped into the boat, and ordered me to go with him (I having been on board the *St. George* to remain till the ship got over the grounds). All I had ever seen or heard of him could not half so clearly prove to me the singular and unbounded zeal of this truly great man. His anxiety in the boat, for nearly six hours, lest the fleet should have sailed before he could get on board one of them, and lest we should not catch the Swedish squadron, is beyond conception. I will quote some of his expressions in his own words. It was extremely cold, and I wished him to put on a great-coat of mine which was in the boat. 'No ; I am not cold : my anxiety for my country will keep me warm. Do you think the fleet has sailed?' 'I should suppose not, my lord.' 'If they have, we will follow them in the boat, Briarly.' The distance to Carlscrona was about fifty leagues. At midnight, however, Lord Nelson reached the *Elephant*, on board which ship he rehoisted his flag." There could not be a stronger proof of zeal than this—an open boat, without provisions of any kind, a stormy season and boisterous sea,—nothing appeared to weigh with him to keep him back. An enemy was, as he supposed, at hand ; and, doubtless, he would have accomplished his object or have lost his life in the attempt.

On the 23rd of April Nelson wrote :—"Affairs bear an aspect of reconciliation with the north, for we are now returning to an anchorage at Copenhagen, having looked at the Swedes in Carlscrona ; for Sir Hyde Parker has received a notification from the Russian minister at Copenhagen, that his master will not go to war with us. I trust all these events will bring about an honourable peace, and allow me to get a little of that repose which my shattered carcase so much wants." One cause which led to this amicable message was probably the death of Paul, which took place on the 24th of

March. Instructions were also received by Sir Hyde Parker from the Admiralty, directing him to suspend operations. The fighting being thus at an end, Nelson was the more desirous of returning to England ; but his wish was set aside in a manner which he was obliged to consider complimentary.

On the 5th of May despatches arrived from England appointing him commander-in-chief, in room of Admiral Sir Hyde Parker. Two days afterwards the fleet was standing out of Kioge Bay – where it had been lying idle for some weeks—and proceeding towards Bornholm, off the end of which island the whole soon anchored. Here the greater part remained, watching the motions of the Swedish fleet in Carlscrona, while Nelson with ten sail of the line departed for Revel. He was not satisfied with amicable Russian promises, and considered that the best mode of putting their sentiments to the test would be by entering one of their ports. He desired peace, and had no apprehension of hostilities. But he had two other objects in view in going to Revel, a desire to ascertain the state of his fleet, and to wait on Paul's successor to the Imperial throne of Russia. He had also a wish to obtain the release of British merchant ships and seamen, unjustly detained by a decree of the late emperor.

Nelson acknowledged the honour of the command conferred upon him ; but in a private letter to Mr. Davison, he said, " A command never was, I believe, more unwelcomely received by any person than by myself. The time was, a few months ago, that I should have felt the honour ; and I really think I should have seen more of the Baltic, the consequence of which I can guess. But nothing, I believe, but change of climate can cure me, and having my mind tranquil."

In a letter to Earl St. Vincent, of the same date, he says : " I am in truth unable to hold the very honourable station you have conferred upon me— Admiral Graves, also, is so ill as to keep his bed. I will have all the English shipping and property restored, but I will do nothing violently. As the business will be settled in a fortnight, I must entreat that some person may come out to take this command." Writing to Mr. Addington, who had stated that, under " all the circumstances, his Majesty had approved of the armistice," Nelson objected to such a conditional approval. " I own myself of opinion," said he, " that every part of the *all* was to the advantage of our

king and country. We knew not of the death of Paul, or a change of sentiments in the court of Russia. . . . My health is gone, and although I
should be happy to try and hold out a month or six weeks longer, yet death
is no respecter of persons. I own, at present, I should not wish to die a
natural death."

On the 11th of May the fleet entered Revel Roads, but the Russians had
left it three days previously, and had proceeded to Cronstadt. Having
anchored, Lord Nelson sent on shore to the Governor-General Sacken, to
inquire whether a salute would be fired, in which case he promised to return
it. After a delay of a day, salutes were given and returned, and Nelson
went on shore at noon, on the 13th, and was received by the governor with
military honours, and with great cordiality by the populace, by whom Paul
had been universally detested. His visit was returned on the 14th, when
General Sacken was accompanied by the Russian minister's son, and several
Cossack officers. In the meanwhile, a letter he had written to the emperor
had been received, and Alexander's ministers, in reply, expressed their surprise at the arrival of a British fleet in a Russian port, and a wish that it
should depart. The most friendly professions were made ; but Lord Nelson's
offer to visit the Russian court was declined, unless he proceeded to St.
Petersburgh in a single ship. The answer to his letter, and the suspicion
thereby implied, roused Nelson's indignation, and he stated that such an in-
sinuation would not have been made had the Russian fleet been then at Revel.
He wrote an immediate rejoinder, and told the court of Petersburgh that
"the word of a British admiral, when given in explanation of any part of his
conduct, was as sacred as that of any sovereign in Europe." It was Lord
Nelson's opinion that, had it been necessary to attack the Russian fleet at
Revel, they might easily have been destroyed by setting fire to the wooden
mole, under which they were lying. A three-decker moored across the mouth
of the harbour would have raked every ship in the dock.

The fleet was kept constantly on the alert, and Nelson took care to obtain
plentiful supplies of fresh water and provisions for the crews of his ships.
Colonel Stewart thus mentions Nelson's habits at this period :—" His hour
of rising was four or five o'clock, and of going to rest about ten ; breakfast
was never later than six, and generally nearer to five o'clock. A midshipman
or two were always of the party, and I have known him send during the

middle watch to invite the little fellows to breakfast with him when relieved. At table with them he would enter into their boyish jokes, and be the most youthful of the party. At dinner he had every officer of the ship in turn, and was both a polite and hospitable host. The whole ordinary business of the fleet was invariably despatched, as it had been by Lord St. Vincent, by eight o'clock. The great command of time which Lord Nelson thus gave himself, and the alertness which this example imparted throughout the fleet, can only be understood by those who witnessed it, or who know the value of early hours."

The Russian frigate *Venus*, having Admiral Tchitchagoff on board, joined the fleet off Bornholm, to which place Nelson had returned on the 19th. The *Venus* had been in search of the fleet for some time, with the answer to certain pacific overtures made by Sir Hyde Parker. "At Rostock," writes Colonel Stewart, " the greatest veneration was shown to the name of Nelson, and some distant inland towns of Mecklenburg sent deputations with their public books of record to have his name written in them by himself. Boats were constantly rowing round the *St. George* with persons of respectability in them, anxious to catch a sight of this illustrious man.

He did not again land whilst in the Baltic ; his health was not good, and his mind was not at ease—with him mind and health invariably sympathised." The *St. George* made the last cruise with Lord Nelson's flag between the 9th and 13th of June, on which latter day despatches from England arrived. In a few days the *Æolus* frigate, having Admiral Sir Charles Morice Pole on board, arrived, to whom, on the 19th of June, Lord Nelson relinquished the command.

Earl St. Vincent's letter on the occasion was very gratifying. He wrote:— " I have the deepest concern at learning from Lieutenant-Colonel Hutchinson that your health has suffered· in so material a degree. To find a proper successor is no easy task; for I never saw the man in our profession, excepting yourself and Troubridge, who possessed the magic art of infusing the same spirit into others which inspired their own actions, exclusive of other talents and habits of business not common to naval characters. . . All agree there is but one Nelson." On quitting the *St. George*, Lord Nelson embarked on board the *Kite* brig, Captain Digby, in which he arrived at

Yarmouth on the 1st of July. His resignation of the command was attended with general regret throughout the fleet.

There can be no question that the dissolution of the northern confederacy was chiefly due to Nelson s indefatigable zeal, and to his successes at Copenhagen. The death of the Czar Paul contributed to the event; but had not the Danes been overawed by the victory of the 2nd of April, French power would have been openly dominant. The death of Paul, and the perseverance of Nelson, occasioned some respect to be paid to the armistice, but it was evident opportunity only was wanted to cause its repudiation.

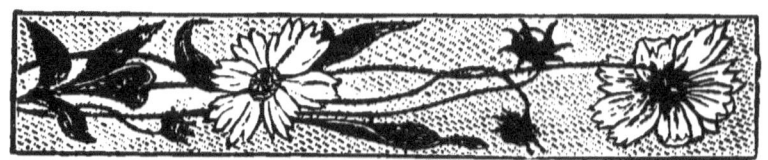

CHAPTER VII.

1801—1803.

DEFEATED in his designs upon the East—a refugee from Egypt—his schemes overthrown chiefly by the vigilance and exertions of the British navy—Bonaparte's rage may be imagined. Like a wounded snake writhing under the blows of its assailant, he knew that an effort must be made in another direction. In the summer of 1801, Bonaparte, now first consul, collected an immense flotilla, and drew together a large army, with which he hoped to strike a blow at England's vitals. Exertions were not wanted on our part to resist the threatened invasion. Earl St. Vincent's plan was a good one, which was to place the whole of the force assembled, for the purpose of averting the meditated attack under the command of some distinguished flag-officer, and no one seemed so eligible as Nelson.

At this time Admiral Skeffington Lutwidge, Nelson's former captain, was commander-in-chief of the Downs station, with whom the new appointment was not to interfere. On the 27th of July, in accordance with the above recommendation, Nelson was ordered to hoist his flag on board the *Unité* frigate at Sheerness. Two days before hoisting his flag, Nelson wrote a most able paper, entitled "Observations on the Defence of the Thames," which proved that he was keenly alive to the task he was about to undertake. It seems highly probable that had the flotillas sailed on their intended service, their destruction would have ensued ere they had got half channel

118

over; and this Bonaparte foresaw. The defeat of divisions of the force by the British frigates and brigs stationed off Boulogne, under Captain Edward Owen, convinced him that a fleet of line-of-battle ships was necessary to escort the flotillas across, and hence his temporary abandonment of the design.

But Nelson, urged in part by his indomitable spirit, and in part by the great wish of the Admiralty to destroy the flotillas in their own port, under took to act upon the offensive. Frequent bombardments took place of Calais, Boulogne, and Gravelines. In the meanwhile Nelson was organising the sea fencibles and volunteer corps upon our coasts, arming river cra' and making every possible preparation for meeting an enemy, from whateve' quarter coming. In a letter, dated August 11, to Earl St. Vincent, he wrote:—"Our active force is perfect, and possesses so much zeal, that I only wish to catch that Bonaparte on the water, either with the *Amazon* or *Medusa*, but himself he would never trust. He would say, '*Allez vous en*,' and not '*Allons, mes amis*,' I hope these French, if they mean to come this year, will come before the 14th of September, beyond which I fear the season will be too much for me." And then, in allusion probably to some suggested attack, he adds:—"I know not at this moment where I had best strike a blow—which I wish to be a very hard one. You have well guessed the place—Flushing; but I must be careful and not cripple our gun-brigs. At Ostend we cannot get at them, therefore I am anxious for our howitzer-boats; but they will not keep pace with my wishes. No person knows of my ideas except Captain Owen, who has long been stationed here, and Captains Bedford and Parker."

In subsequent letters Nelson wrote dubiously as to the propriety of an attack:—"I now come to consider of an attack—Flushing is my grand object; but so many obstacles are in the way, and *the risk is so great* of the loss of some vessels, that under all circumstances I could hardly venture without a consultation with you, and an arranged plan with the Board's orders. . . . I purpose, *if it can be done*, to take all the gun-vessels outside the pier of Boulogne—I should like your approbation. This boat warfare is not exactly congenial to my feelings," &c. All these expressions sound strange when coming from Nelson, and it is clear his judgment was averse to the operation. It was, however, at length decided upon, that an attack with the boats should be made on the Boulogne flotilla. The French were well prepared—their vessels, which were crowded with troops, were admirably calculated for defence, and a successful attempt upon them was scarcely within the reach of possibility.

A few of the devoted officers and noble assailants returned to tell the dismal story of their defeat; and Nelson, with what pain few can describe, made his official report to the Admiralty. It was dated, "Medusa, off Boulogne, August 16th, 1801.—Having judged it proper to attempt bringing off the enemy's flotilla moored in front of Boulogne, I directed the attack to be made by four divisions of boats for boarders, under the command of Captains Somerville, Cotgrave, Jones, and Parker, and a division of howitzer boats under Captain Conn. The boats put off from the Medusa at half-past eleven o'clock last night, in the best possible order, and before one o'•lock this morning the firing began, and I had, from the judgment of the officers and the zeal and gallantry of every man, the most perfect confidence of complete success. But the darkness of the night, with the tide and half-tide, separated the divisions; and from all not arriving at the same happy moment with Captain Parker is to be attributed the failure of success. But I beg to be perfectly understood, that not the smallest blame attaches itself to any person; for, although the divisions did not arrive together, yet each (except the fourth division, which could not be got up before day) made a successful attack on that part of the enemy they fell in with, and actually took possession of many brigs and flats, and cut their cables; but many of them being aground, and the moment of the battle ceasing on board of them, the vessels were filled with volleys upon volleys of musketry, the enemy being perfectly regardless of their own men, who must have suffered equally with ours. It was therefore impossible to remain on board, even to burn them; but allow me to say, who have seen much service this war, that more determined, persevering courage I never witnessed, and that nothing but the impossibility of being successful, from the causes I have mentioned, could have prevented me from having to congratulate their lordships.

" But although, in value, the loss of such gallant and good men is incalculable, yet in point of numbers it has fallen short of my expectations. I must also beg leave to state that greater zeal and ardent desire to distinguish themselves by an attack on the enemy was never shown than by all the captains, officers, and crews of the different descriptions of vessels under my command. The commanders of the *Hunter* and *Greyhound*, revenue cutters, went in their boats in the most handsome and gallant manner to the attack. Amongst the many gallant men wounded, I have, with the deepest regret, to place the name of my gallant friend and able assistant, Captain Edward T. Parker, also my flag-lieutenant, Frederick Langford, who has served with me many years ; they were wounded in attempting to board the French commodore.

" To Captain Gore, of the *Medusa*, I feel the highest obligations ; and when their lordships look at the loss of the *Medusa* on this occasion, they will agree with me, that the honour of my flag, and the cause of their king and country, could never have been placed in more gallant hands. Captain Bedford, of the *Leyden*, with Captain Gore, very handsomely volunteered their services to serve under a master and commander ; but I did not think it fair to the latter, and I only mention it to mark the zeal of those officers. From the nature of the attack, only a few prisoners were made ; a lieutenant, eight seamen, and eight soldiers, are all they brought off. Herewith I send the report of the several commanders of divisions, and a return of killed and wounded.—I have the honour to be, &c.   Captain Somerville was the senior master and commander employed."

To Earl St. Vincent he wrote :—" My dear Lord, I am sorry to tell you that I have not succeeded in bringing out or destroying the enemy's flotilla moored in the mouth of the harbour of Boulogne. The most astonishing bravery was evinced by many of our officers and men, and Captains Somerville, Cotgrave, and Parker exerted themselves to the utmost. We have lost many brave officers and men ; upwards of 100 killed and wounded. Dear little Parker's thigh is very much shattered ; I have fears for his life. Langford shot through the leg. The loss has been heavy and the object was great. The flotilla, brigs and flats, were moored by the bottom to the shore, and to each other by chains ; therefore, although several of them were carried, yet the heavy fire of musketry from the shore, which over-looked them, forced our people to leave them, without being able, as I am told, to set them on fire. No person can be blamed for sending them to the attack but myself ; I knew the difficulty of the undertaking, therefore I ventured to ask your opinion. Your kind letter I received half an hour before the attack ; but, my dear lord, although I disapprove of unnecessary consultation as much as any man, yet [being] close to the Admiralty, I should not feel myself justified in risking our ships through the channels of Flushing without buoys and pilots, without a consultation with such men as your lordship, and also I believe you would think an order absolutely necessary.   But that must stand fast, for both *Leyden* and *Medusa* have lost all their best men—none else of course being sent.

" Captain Somerville, whom I never saw till a few days before, showed all the courage and good conduct which was possible, and succeeded completely in the fighting part of the business.   Conn, in the command of the howitzer boats, did everything which was possible ; indeed, all behaved well, and it was their misfortune to be sent on a service which the precautions of the enemy rendered impossible to succeed in.   After all this (sorrow for me), my health is not improved ; my fever is very severe this morning. The *Medusa* cannot move till she gets some good men ; nor, I believe, the *Leyden.*   The *Unité* would complete both these ships, taking some marines. This ship has lost seventeen killed and thirty wounded, with two lieutenants, master, mids., etc.   Young Cathcart behaved most exceedingly well ; he saved Parker from either being killed or made a prisoner ; for every man in Parker's flat boat being killed or wounded, his boat drifted from the brig alongside a flat full of men."

The mortification of Nelson at this lamentable failure, the blame of which he took upon himself, was heightened by the loss of a promising young friend, Captain Thornborough Parker, who died of his wounds ; and it is questionable whether Teneriffe or Boulogne was felt as the greater of the two calamities.   He, however, continued to keep his flag flying till the close of the year.   No one could attribute blame to Nelson, for his arrangements had been all that forethought could suggest.   He was consoled by letters from Earl St. Vincent, and comforted by the assurance that he deserved the success which had been denied him.

The signature of the preliminaries of peace put a period, for a time, to his active labours, and he retired to repose beneath his hard-earned laurels, and to the enjoyment of domestic happiness, at the seat which he had purchased at Merton, in Surrey.   Here his chief amusement was angling in the Wandle. His income was too limited to admit of him indulging in society, to which, also, his retiring habits were averse. His total income from pensions and half-pay amounted to about £3,400 a year; out of which he allowed Lady Nelson £1,800 a year, and £200 to the widow of his brother Maurice, together with £150 for the education of his orphan children. He had also to pay £500 a year for interest upon borrowed money. His income, therefore, thus narrowed—mainly, it is true, in consequence of his separation from Lady Nelson—was very scanty; but it sufficed for his wants, which were few. His affability, and the gentleness of his manners gained him the heart of every one who approached him, while his unostentatious charity was the theme of general admiration.

Though thus reposing for a short interval after the more arduous labours of his professional career, he punctually attended to his duties as a peer of the realm. His natural diffidence prevented him from recording his sentiments on many of the subjects that came before the House for discussion, but whatever he said was to the purpose, and expressed with such energy and ability, that he always commanded the attention and respect of the House.

When Earl of St. Vincent, on the 30th of October, moved the thanks of the House of Lords to Sir James Saumarez, for his distinguished conduct against the combined French and Spanish fleet off Algeziras, the motion was warmly seconded by Nelson. He said, "he could not give a silent vote to a motion that so cordially had his consent. He had the honour to be the friend of Sir James Saumarez. The noble earl at the head of the Admiralty had selected that great officer to watch the French in that important quarter, and the noble earl had not been deceived in his choice. He would assert, that a greater action was never fought than*that of Sir James Saumarez. The gallant admiral had before that action undertaken an enterprise, which none but the most gallant officer and the bravest seaman could have attempted. He had failed through an accident, by the falling of the wind; for he ventured to say, if that had not failed him, Sir James Saumarez would have captured the French fleet. The promptness with which Sir James refitted, the spirit with which he attacked a superior force after his recent disaster, and the masterly conduct of the action, he did not think were ever surpassed." His lordship entered very much into the detail of the action, and said, " that the merit of Sir James Saumarez would be less wondered at, when the school in which he was educated was considered by their lordships. He was educated at first under Lord Hood, and afterwards under the noble earl near him (Lord St. Vincent)." His lordship then gave an account of some of the memorable services of Sir James Saumarez when a captain, and concluded by apologizing to the house for the trouble he had given their lordships.

On the 3rd of November following, when the preliminaries of peace with France were under consideration in the House of Lords, and ministers were censured for consenting to give up Malta, the noble admiral made some observations relative to the importance of that island. He said, "that when he was sent down the Mediterranean, Malta was in the hands of the French, and on his return from Aboukir it was his first object to blockade the island, because he deemed it an invaluable service to rescue it from their possession. In any other view it was not of much consequence, being at too great a distance from Toulon to watch the enemy's fleet from that port in time of war." A few days afterwards, when Lord Hobart rose to move the thanks of the house to the naval officers and seamen who had co-operated in the conquest of Egypt, Lord Nelson said, that " the service of Egypt was of a double nature, yet of equal importance ; it fell to the lot of the army to fight, and of the navy to labour ; they had equally performed their duty, and were equally entitled to thanks."

Earl St. Vincent, in 1802, projected a plan for the correction of abuses committed by certain boards employed in the naval department of the public service, and by prize-agents, on which occasion Lord Nelson stood forth as his zealous supporter. On the second reading of the bill for appointing commissioners to inquire into these abuses, on the 21st of December previously, he spoke to the following effect :—" In the absence of my noble friend who is at the head of the Admiralty, I think it my duty to say a few words to their lordships, in regard to a bill, of which the objects have an express reference to the interests of my profession as a seaman. It undoubtedly originated in the feeling of the Admiralty, that they have not the power to remedy certain abuses which they perceive to be the most injurious to the public service. Every man knows that there are such abuses ; I hope there is no one among us who would not gladly do all that can be constitutionally effected to correct them. Yet, if I had heard of any objection of weight urged against the measure in the present Bill, I should certainly have hesitated to do anything to promote its progress through the forms of this house. And truly, my lords, if the bill be thus superior to all objection, I can affirm that the necessities, the wrongs of those who are employed in the naval service of their country, most loudly call for the redress which it proposes. From the highest admiral in the service to the poorest cabin boy that walks the street, there is not one but may be in distress, with large sums of wages due to him, of which he shall by no diligence of request be able to obtain payment : not one whose entreaties will be readily answered with aught but insult at the proper places for his application, if he come not with particular recommendations to a preference. From the highest admiral to the meanest seaman, whatever may be the sums of prize-money due to him, no man can tell when he may securely call any part of it his own. A man may have forty thousand pounds due to him in prize-money, and yet may be dismissed without a shilling, if he ask for it at the proper office, without particular recommendation. Are these things to be tolerated ? Is it for the interest, is it for the honour of the country that they should not be as speedily as possible redressed ? I should be as unwilling as any man to give an overweening preference to the interests of my own profession. But I cannot help thinking that, under all the circumstances of the business, your lordships will be strongly disposed to advance this bill into a law, as speedily as may be consistent with the order of your proceedings, and with due prudence of deliberation."

One of the circumstances which had weighed heavily upon Nelson's spirits was occasioned by his venerable father, for whom he had always entertained much affection, and who had been deluded into the belief that Nelson's passion for Lady Hamilton was criminal. The old man had, therefore, become estranged from his son, but having satisfied himself that, however absurd and romantic the attachment really was, he had been deceived as to its true character, a reconciliation took place—an event which contributed much to Nelson's happiness. A few months afterwards Mr. Nelson died at the age of seventy-nine.

The short peace now gave a little breathing time to the belligerent nations, and news having arrived of our successes in Egypt, the usual compliment was paid by the city of London to the army and navy. Nelson had never been able to divest his mind of the slight cast upon the hard-fought battle of Copenhagen, and impelled by his feelings, he addressed a letter to the Lord Mayor upon the subject. "The smallest services rendered by the army and navy to the country," he wrote, "have always been noticed by the great city of London, with one exception—the glorious second of April." His letter vigorously set forth the advantages gained by the victory, but the citizens having had no opportunity of seeing the prizes, could not, or probably would not, understand that an important battle had been fought. Another grievance connected with the Copenhagen victory was the withholding of gold medals. In writing to Earl St. Vincent upon the subject, Nelson said, "he would not give it up, to be made an English duke." But the medal was never granted, neither was any cause assigned for the omission. It is too much to be feared that some unaccountable jealousy occasioned the refusal; and this supposition took such a strong hold upon Nelson's sensitive mind, that it led to a coolness between Lord St. Vincent and himself which was never wholly removed.

Early in 1803 Sir William Hamilton died. "He expired," says Southey, "in his wife's arms, holding Nelson by the hand, and almost in his last words left her to his protection, requesting him that he would see justice done her by the government, as he knew what she had done for the country. He left him her portrait in enamel, calling him his dearest friend,—the most virtuous, loyal, and truly brave character he had ever known. The codicil containing this bequest concluded with these words :—' God bless him, and shame fall on those who do not say, Amen.' "

CHAPTER VIII.

COMMANDER-IN-CHIEF IN THE MEDITERRANEAN.—PURSUIT OF THE FRENCH—DEATH AT TRAFALGAR.

1803—1805.

ON the 16th May, 1803, the tocsin of war again sounded, and Nelson's services were once more in requisition ; and on the 20th, his flag being hoisted on board the *Victory*, he sailed for the Mediterranean, to take command of the fleet. The immediate service upon which he was engaged was the blockade of the French fleet in Toulon. Nothing of importance happened to break the monotony of this employment for the space of nearly fourteen months. Capes Sepet and Sicie were eternally figuring before him, broken only by an occasional resort to Pulla Bay for water. Every inducement was offered to the enemy to come out, but in vain. None but those who have been engaged on such a service can imagine its wearisomeness. A few prizes were taken from time to time, but upon the whole nothing could be more trying to the patience of so active-minded a man as Nelson.

On the 24th May, 1804, Lord Nelson ordered Rear-Admiral Campbell, in the 84-gun ship *Canopus*, with the *Donegal*, Captain Sir Richard Strachan, and the *Amazon* frigate, Captain William Parker, to reconnoitre the outer road of Toulon. This service was boldly performed by the squadron, which remained for some hours just out of gunshot of the batteries. While thus engaged, two French 84-gun ships, three of 74 guns, three 44-gun frigates, and a corvette, got under way, and stood out towards them. The frigates, and the *Scipion*, of 74 guns, gained considerably, and the headmost of the former opened fire on the *Donegal*. This was borne patiently for some time, but at length the *Donegal* luffed up and fired a broadside, which checked the ardour of the enemy. Some shot from the *Canopus* at the same time retarded the progress of the *Scipion*. The force of the French fleet was so far superior, that it would have been madness to hazard an engagement. The enemy continued to follow under a crowd of sail ; but fearing lest he should be decoyed into the jaws of the fleet, then about nine leagues distant, relinquished the chase.

On the 13th June, another skirmish took place off Toulon with a division of the French fleet, when Admiral Latouche Treville commanded. The occasion was the cover of three French frigates entering the port ; and, having effected this object, Latouche Treville hauled to the wind, and returned to Toulon covered with glory, alleging that he had chased the whole British fleet off the port. M. Latouche's idle boast, childish as it was, gave Nelson much uneasiness, and induced him to send to England a copy of the log of the *Victory*, to prove how untrue were the French admiral's statements. Shortly afterwards M. Latouche died, the French papers said, from fatigue in walking so frequently to the signal-post at Cape Sepet.

For his conduct during this long interval of fruitless expectation, Nelson received the thanks of the Corporation of London, which elicited the following spirited reply :—

" This day I am honoured with your lordship's letter of April 9th, trans-mitting me the resolutions of the Corporation of London, thanking me as commanding the fleet blockading Toulon. I do assure your lordship that there is not that man breathing who sets a higher value upon the thanks of his fellow-citizens of London than myself ; but I should feel as much ashamed to receive them for a particular service marked in the resolution, if I felt that I did not come within that line of service, as I should feel hurt at having a great victory passed over without notice. I beg to inform your lordship that the port of Toulon has never been blockaded by me ; quite the reverse : every opportunity has been offered the enemy to put to sea, for it is there that we hope to realise the hopes and expectations of our country, and I trust that they will not be disappointed. Your lordship will judge of my feelings upon seeing that all the junior flag-officers of other fleets, and even some of the captains, have received the thanks of the Corporation of London, whilst the junior flag-officers of the Mediterranean fleet are entirely omitted. I own it has struck me very forcibly ; for where the information of the junior flag-officers and captains of other fleets was obtained, the same information could have been given of the flag-officers of this fleet and the captains ; and it is my duty to state that more able and zealous flag-officers and captains do not grace the British navy than those I have the honour and happiness to command. It likewise appears, my lord, a most extraordinary circumstance, that Rear-Admiral Sir Richard Bickerton should have been, as second in command in the Mediterranean fleet, twice passed over by the Corporation of London ; once after the Egyptian expedition, when the first and third in command were thanked, and now again. Consciousness of high desert, instead of neglect, made the rear-admiral resolve to let the matter rest until he could have an opportunity personally to call upon the Lord Mayor to account for such an extraordinary omission ; but from this second omission I owe it to that excellent officer not to pass it by.

"And I do assure your lordship, that the constant, zealous, and cordial support I have had in my command from both Rear-Admiral Sir Richard Bickerton and Rear-Admiral Campbell has been such as calls forth all my thanks and admiration. We have shared together the constant attention of being more than fourteen months at sea, and are ready to share the dangers and glory of a day of battle ; therefore, it is impossible that I can ever allow myself to be separated in thanks from such supporters."

On the 11th of September, a seaman of the *Victory* fell from the forecastle into the sea. On hearing the cry, Mr. Edward Flin, a volunteer, jumped after him from the quarter-deck, and, notwithstanding the extreme darkness of the night, had the good fortune to save the man. The next morning Lord Nelson sent for Mr. Flin, and presented him with a lieutenant's commission, appointing him to the *Bittern* sloop-of-war.

Nelson's state of health at this period was very distressing. Writing to Dr. Baird, physician of the Navy, after describing the general good health of the seamen in the fleet, he says :—" I have had a sort of rheumatic fever,

5

they tell me. I have felt the blood gushing up the left side of my head, and the moment it covers the brain I am fast asleep. I am now better of that, but with violent pain in my side. Mr. Magrath, whom I admire every day I live, gives me excellent remedies; but we must lose such men from our service if the army goes on encouraging medical men whilst we do nothing."

Hostilities at length commenced between Great Britain and Spain. The ostensible cause of the war was the seizure of four Spanish frigates, laden with treasure, by a British squadron; but, in point of fact, the rupture had long before been decided upon, and the treasure intercepted was principally intended to furnish means for the French armament. This war would have enabled Nelson to replenish his own, and his officers' empty coffers; but, as if the Admiralty had determined he should have all the bitters without the sweets of the service, another admiral—Sir John Orde—was despatched from England with a small squadron, purposely to reap the rich fruits of the rupture. "I did fancy," he wrote, "but it must have been a dream—an idle dream—that I had done my country service; and thus they use me. And under what circumstances, and with what pointed aggravation! Yet, if I know my own thoughts, it is not for myself, or on my own account, that I feel the sting and the disappointment. No! It is for my brave officers, for my noble-minded friends and comrades. Such a gallant set of fellows! Such a band of brothers! My heart swells at the thought of them."

The fleet, under Lord Nelson, in January, 1805, was lying at anchor in Madalena Harbour, Sardinia, having left the *Active* and *Seahorse* frigates, Captains R. H. Moubray and Courtenay Boyle, to watch the enemy in Toulon. Lord Nelson had had information for some time previously that the French were embarking a considerable number of troops, but the destination of their fleet was a profound secret.

On the 18th the French fleet sailed out of Toulon, and the *Active* and *Seahorse* hastened to convey the news to Madalena, which harbour they reached on the 19th. At the time it was blowing a gale from the N.W.; but at six that evening Nelson's fleet was under way, and running through the narrow passage between Biche and Sardinia. From the position of the enemy when lost sight of, it was supposed they were bound round the southern end of Sardinia. Nelson beat about the coast of Sicily for ten days—the weather had been very stormy. He could not obtain any tidings of the enemy. Finding Sardinia, Naples, and Sicily, unmolested, he concluded Egypt to be their destination—and for Egypt he accordingly steered. Still foiled in his pursuit, his anxiety was most painful, and not knowing what other course to take, he bore up for Malta. Here he learnt that the enemy he was in search of had sustained much damage in the gale, and had returned to Toulon. He was here, also, informed that the French fleet had taken on board a great number of saddles and muskets, which induced him to believe Egypt to be their destination. The fact of the French fleet's having put back in consequence of a storm, surprised Nelson. "They are not accustomed," said he, "to a Gulf of Lyons gale. We have buffeted them for one-and-twenty months, and have not carried away a spar." During the chase every ship was clear for action day and night.

The fleet regained its station off Toulon on the 4th of April, having, for several weeks previously, sustained a series of gales. Here the *Phœbe* frigate gave information that the French fleet, of eleven sail of the line, seven frigates, and two brigs, under Admiral Villeneuve, had sailed from Toulon on the 31st of March. When last seen they were steering for the African coast. Nelson's first object was to cover the channel between Sardinia and Barbary ; and, having satisfied himself that Villeneuve had not gone to Egypt, he bore up for Palermo. It was the 11th of April before he could make up his mind that the French had left the Mediterranean, when he made all the haste he could to get to the westward. The wind, however, was dead against him, which added a hundredfold to Nelson's misery. Five days elapsed ere he gained any definite information. A neutral vessel which he then fell in with, told him that the French had been seen off Cape de Gatt on the 7th. He afterwards learnt that they had passed Gibraltar on the 8th. Still the hard-hearted westerly wind impeded his progress. "This ill-luck," said he, writing to Captain Ball, "will go near to kill me ; but as these are times for exertion, I must not be cast down, whatever I may feel." It was not until the 30th of April that Nelson's fleet reached Gibraltar, and then, owing to the strong adverse wind, he could not get through the Straits. He anchored in Mazari Bay, on the Barbary shore, where he obtained supplies of water and fresh provisions from Tetuan. On the 5th of May, taking advantage of an easterly wind, he pushed through the gulf, hoping to hear something of the enemy from

Sir John Orde. In writing to the Admiralty, he said:—"If nothing is heard of them, I shall think the rumours which have been spread are true, that their object is the West Indies; and, in that case, I think it my duty to follow them." When we consider Nelson's state of mind at that period —his health and spirits weighed down by continual fatigue and anxiety, it is surprising to find how well he bore up, and that he was able, in despite of every obstacle, to undertake the arduous service. "I am going," he wrote to Sir John Acton, "to the West Indies, where the enemy have twenty-four sail of the line. My force is very, very inferior. I only take ten with me, and I only expect to be joined by six."

On the 10th of May he proceeded to Lagos Bay, whence on his arrival he wrote to Admiral Campbell:—"Here we are clearing Sir John Orde's transports which I found in Lagos Bay, completing ourselves to five months; and to-morrow I start for the West Indies. Disappointment has worn me to a skeleton, and I am in good truth very, very far from well. Sir Richard Bickerton remains in the Mediterranean, and Admiral Knight, reports say, is to command at Gibraltar. He is at present off Lisbon with the convoy of troops. I wish he would come here; but he has been deceived by false information, that the combined squadrons were still in Cadiz—I wish they were: but I am sorry to believe they are now in the West Indies, or just off."

Nelson's attention was now directed to the West Indies; but although auxious beyond description, there was no hurry or distraction of thought, Everything was weighed with the coolest judgment, and provided against with the utmost forethought. On the 11th he despatched the *Martin* sloop. Captain R. H. Savage, with a letter to Lord Seaforth at Barbadoes; and on the same day Rear-Admiral Knight, with the expected convoy of 5,000 troops, passed towards the Straits. Nelson, in his letter, requested Lord Seaforth, in case Rear-Admiral Cochrane should not be at Barbadoes, to open the official letter, and recommended its being forwarded on as expeditiously as possible. He also earnestly begged that an embargo might be laid on all vessels at Barbadoes, that the enemy might not be apprised of his approach. Before sailing he addressed a few lines to Lord Sidmouth. "My lot," said Nelson, "seems to have been hard, and the enemy's most fortunate; but it may turn. Patience and perseverance will do much."

On the 15th of May the fleet reached Madeira ; and the next day a vessel, having the appearance of an enemy's cruiser, was chased for a short time without effect. The greatest exertion was employed to make an expeditious passage ; and Nelson calculated on gaining eight or ten days on the enemy.

On the 29th of May, the fleet being near Barbadoes, the *Amazon* was ordered on ahead, to prepare whatever naval force there might be in Carlisle Bay, to join Lord Nelson on his approach, as he did not intend anchoring, but to proceed at once to Martinique.

On crossing the tropics the following incident occurred, for the narration of which we are indebted to Rear-Admiral Pasco, then a lieutenant of the *Victory.* To relieve the monotony of the chase, Nelson permitted the tars to get up their nautical entertainment, the scene of which is properly confined to crossing the equator. Neptune, however, came on board in fullblown grandeur, attended by an innumerable train and the lovely Amphitrite, and was duly presented to the admiral, who, according to the fashion on such occasions, asked the news of his sea godship. The blunt personifier of the sea deity, although sadly wanting in tact, gave no very wide answer. Nelson asked him what had become of the French fleet, and whether he should overtake the enemy—to which Neptune replied that he had boarded the French fleet three days ago, but that the French admiral, hearing Nelson was in pursuit, had altered his course and gone back again. The answer of the tar overcame Nelson's philosophy, and he turned upon his heel and walked dejected into his cabin. Had Neptune given him a promise of overtaking the enemy, it would have been much more conducive to the harmony of the day.

On the 3rd of June intelligence was received of the enemy being in the West Indies, from two British merchant ships ; and on the 4th the fleet arrived at Barbadoes. Nelson lost no time in writing to the Admiralty. "I arrived off here," he said, "at noon this day, where I found Rear-Admiral Cochrane in the *Northumberland*, and the *Spartiate* is just joining. There is not a doubt but that Tobago and Trinidad are the enemy's objects ; and although I am anxious in the extreme to get at their eighteen sail of the line, yet as Sir W. Myers has offered to embark himself with 2,000 troops, I cannot refuse such a handsome offer. I am now working to an anchorage, and I hope that we shall have sailed before six hours are over, with the general and troops."

The troops were embarked that same evening, and on the morning of the 5th the fleet sailed from Barbadoes, consisting of twelve sail of the line, four frigates, three sloops, and four smaller vessels. The *Curieux* brig, Captain Bettesworth, was detached to look into Tobago for information; and a vessel was sent to General Prevost at Dominica. Colonel Shipley, of the Engineers, was also directed to communicate with the nearest post on Trinidad, and ascertain the situation of the enemy. The British fleet stood to the southward with fine breezes all night. Nelson, on account of the strong lee currents which almost constantly run there, had been recommended to steer south by east from Barbadoes. On the 6th the fleet arrived off Great Courland Bay, Tobago; and Captain Henderson, of the *Pheasant* sloop, was directed to proceed with all expedition to Trinidad, with Sir W. Myers' letters, and seek for information as to whether the enemy were in the Gulf of Paria.

"At Tobago all was bustle and apparent uncertainty, when, in addition, the following singular occurrence took place. A merchant, particularly anxious to ascertain whether the fleet was that of a friend or an enemy, had prevailed on his clerk, with whom he had also agreed respecting signals, to embark in a schooner and stand towards it; and it unfortunately happened that the very signal made by the clerk corresponded with the affirmative signal which had been agreed on by Colonel Shipley, *of the enemy being at Trinidad*. It was the close of the day, and no opportunity occurred of discovering the mistake. An American merchant brig also had been spoken with the same day by the *Curieux*, probably sent to mislead, whose master reported that he had been boarded a few days before by the French fleet off Grenada, standing towards the Boccas of Trinidad. No doubts were any longer entertained, the news flew throughout the British squadron, the ships were ready for action before daybreak, and Nelson anticipated a second Aboukir in the Bay of Paria. If further confirmation was necessary, it appeared in the seeming conflagration of one of our outposts at daylight, and the party retreating towards the citadel. The admiral and officers of his squadron, after such corroboration, felt it difficult to believe the evidence of their senses, when, on entering the Gulf of Paria on the 7th, no enemy was to be seen, nor had any been there! The intelligence from St. Lucia, the corroborating accounts met with at Barbadoes, the American's report off Tobago, the schooner's signal, and conflagration of the outpost, were all false or delusive ; and had contributed to draw the fleet so far to lee-ward, that it could not, as it would seem, fetch to windward of Grenada."

At daylight on the 8th of June an advice-boat arrived from Barbadoes, with letters from Captain J. W. Maurice, announcing the capture of the Diamond Rock, and that the combined fleet was still at Martinique, but that the French commodore had told him the Ferrol squadron, consisting of six sail of French and eight Spanish, had arrived in Fort Royal Bay on the 4th. Nelson, writing to Lord Seaforth, said, "The information from St. Lucia of the combined squadron having been off that island to windward must have been very incorrect. I have my doubts respecting the certainty of the arrival of the Ferrol squadron, as I have always understood that nothing could pass in or out of Fort Royal without being seen ; but, power-ful as their force may be, they shall not with impunity make any great attacks. Mine is compact, theirs must be unwieldy ; and although a very pretty fiddle, I don't believe that either Gravina or Villeneuve know how to play upon it."

On entering the Gulf of Paria, Nelson found, to his sorrow, the fallacy of the reports. He had, from the first, mistrusted them, and although his doubts had been based upon conjecture, they proved to be correct. He, however, immediately exerted his energies to remedy the error. Captain Maurice's intelligence leading him to believe that an attack would be made on Grenada, Nelson immediately shaped a course for that island, where he arrived on the 9th. Here he received a letter from General Prevost, stating that the enemy had passed Dominica on the 6th, standing to the northward. On the 8th they passed to leeward of Antigua, and captured a convoy of sugar-laden ships homeward bound, which had left St. John's during the preceding night. Having on his passage communicated with Dominica, Nelson was off Montserrat on the 11th, and at sun-set of the 12th anchored in St. John's, Antigua, to disembark the troops.

From this place he sent the *Curieux* to England with his despatches, among which was the following letter to his friend the Duke of Clarence :— " Your royal highness will easily conceive the misery I am feeling, at hitherto having missed the French fleet ; and entirely owing to false information sent from St. Lucia, which arrived at Barbadoes the evening of June 3rd. This caused me to embark Sir William Myers and 2,000 troops, and to proceed to Tobago and Trinidad.   But for that false information, I should have been off Fort Royal as they were putting to sea, and our battle most probably would have been fought on the spot where the brave Rodney beat De Grasse.   I am rather inclined to believe they are pushing for Europe to get out of our way ; and the moment my mind is made up, I shall stand for the Straits' mouth.   But I must not move, after having saved these colonies and 200 and upwards of sugar-laden ships, until I feel sure they are gone.   We saw, about 100 leagues to the westward of Madeira, a vessel which I took to be a French corvette, that watched us two days ; but we could not take her.   She, I hear, gave Gravina notice of our approach, and that probably hastened his movements ; however, I feel I have done my duty to the very utmost of my abilities."

In the course of eight days Nelson had averted from our West India colonies that plunder and havoc with which they had been threatened.   In this space of time he had embarked and disembarked 2,000 troops, had entered the Gulf of Paria, and surmounting the various obstacles that retarded his progress, had shown his power to every island from Trinidad to St. Kitt's.   He now resolved again to pursue them across the Atlantic. Some thought the enemy would return, and attack Barbadoes ; some that they would go to St. John's, Porto Rico, be there joined by reinforcements, and proceed to Jamaica, whilst others believed they would call at the Havanna for such Spanish ships as were ready, and sweep the coast of Nova Scotia and Newfoundland.   " I hear all," said Nelson, "and even feel obliged, for all is meant as kindness to me, that I should get at them.   In this diversity of opinions, I may as well follow my own, which is, that the Spaniards are gone to the Havanna, and that the French will either stand for Cadiz or Toulon—I feel most inclined to the latter place ; and then they may fancy that they will get to Egypt without any interruption."

On the 13th of June Nelson sailed from Antigua with eleven line of battle ships, including the *Spartiate*, Captain Sir F. Laforey ; confidently believing that he should be able by superior management to reach Europe before the combined fleet.   Whenever opportunities offered of going on board the

Victory without causing delay to the squadron, he would have the captains of the different ships on board to consult with him.

In one of these unreserved conversations he said, " I am thankful that the enemy has been driven from the West India islands with so little loss to our country. I had made up my mind to great sacrifices, for I had determined, notwithstanding his vast superiority, to stop his career, and to put it out of his power to do any further mischief. Yet, do not imagine I am one of those hot-brained people who fight at immense disadvantage, without an adequate object. My object is partly gained if we meet them. We shall find them not less than eighteen, I rather think twenty sail of the line, and therefore do not be surprised if I should not fall on them immediately. We won't part without a battle. I think they will be glad to let me alone, if I will let them alone, which I will do either till we approach the shores of Europe, or they give me an advantage too tempting to be resisted."

The fleet continued standing to the northward, but without any intelligence of the enemy. Writing on the 16th June to the Admiralty, Nelson thus expressed himself :—" I may be mistaken in thinking that the enemy's fleet is gone to Europe, and yet I cannot bring myself to think otherwise, notwithstanding the variety of opinions which different people of good judgment form. But I have called every circumstance that I have heard of their proceedings before me. I have considered the approaching season, the sickly state of their troops and ships, the means and time for defence which have been given to our islands, and the certainty with which the enemy mu expect the arrival of our reinforcements, and therefore, if they were not able to make an attack for the first three weeks after they had reached the West Indies, they could not hope for greater success when our means of resistance had increased, and their means of defence were diminished, and it should be considered that the enemy will not give me credit for quitting the West Indies for this month to come. . . . My opinion is firm as a rock, that some counter-orders, or an inability to perform any service in these seas, have made them resolve to proceed directly to Europe, sending the Spanish ships to the Havanna."

On the 18th, the *Amazon* reported having spoke a schooner, who had seen on the preceding Saturday, at sunset, a fleet, consisting of twenty-two sail of ships of war, steering to the northward. The enemy by computation bore N.E. by N. eighty-seven leagues. On the 19th, the *Martin* was detached to Gibraltar, and the *Décade* to Lisbon. Nelson's anxiety and depression of spirits was very great.

On the 21st, an entry appears in his diary:—"Midnight, nearly calm, saw three planks, which, 1 think, came from the French fleet. Very miserable, which is very foolish." At the beginning of July the wind shifted to the north-east, with rain. "It appears hard," exclaimed he, "but as it pleases God: he knows what is best for us poor weak mortals." No circumstance of moment occurred during the remainder of the voyage, but Nelson for a considerable time calculated the daily supposed track and position of the enemy.

On Wednesday, 17th of July, the fleet got sight of Cape St. Vincent, making the whole run from Barbuda 3,459 miles. The distance traversed in the run from Cape St. Vincent to Barbadoes was 3,227 miles, so that the run back was only 232 miles more than the passage out, averaging nearly 112 miles a day. On the 18th, being in want of provisions, the fleet steered for Gibraltar; and at ten, Vice-Admiral Collingwood, mistaking the British fleet for the enemy, passed to the northward. Next day the fleet anchored at Gibraltar. On the 20th, Nelson remarked in his diary, " I went on shore for the first time since the 16th of June, 1803, and from having my foot out of the *Victory* two years wanting ten days."

On the 21st, the ships were busily employed getting ready for sea, and Lord Nelson sent home his despatches in a merchant brig.

The fleet unmoored on the 22nd, and at 8h. P.M., anchored in Mazari Bay to water. On the 24th the *Décade* joined, but without information of the enemy. The fleet weighed at noon, and stood for Ceuta. On the next day the *Termagant* joined, with an account that the combined fleet had been seen by the *Curieux* on the 19th, standing to the northward.

Having passed the Straits, and communicated with Collingwood, Nelson proceeded off Cape St. Vincent. "And now a circumstance occurred, which, though trifling in itself, marked the extraordinary mind of Nelson. An American merchant ship, spoken by one of the frigates, had fallen in a little to the westward of the *Azores* with an armed vessel, having the appearance of a privateer dismasted, and which had evident marks of having been set fire to and run on board by another ship, the impression of whose stem had penetrated the top sides. The crew had forsaken her, and the fire most probably had gone out of its own accord,

 " In the cabin had been found a log-book and a few seamen's jackets, which were given to the officer and taken on board the *Victory* ; and with these, the admiral endeavoured to explain the mystery, and to discover some further intelligence of the enemy. The log-book, which closed with this remark, ' Two large ships in the W.N.W.,' showed, in his opinion, that the abandoned vessel had been a Liverpool privateer cruising off the Western Islands. In the leaves of this log-book, a small scrap of dirty paper was found filled with figures, which no one could make anything of but Lord Nelson, who, immediately, on seeing it, remarked, ' They are French characters.' After an attentive examination, he said, ' I can unravel the whole : this privateer had been chased and taken by the two ships that were seen in the W.N.W. The prize-master, who had been put on board in a hurry, omitted to take with him his reckoning, there is none in the log-book ; and this dirty scrap of paper, which none of you could make anything of, contains his work for the number of days since the privateer last set Corvo, with an unaccounted-for run, which I take to have been the chase, in his endeavour to find out his situation by back-reckonings. The jackets I find to be the manufacture of France, which prove the enemy was in possession of the privateer ; and I conclude, by some mismanagement she was run on board of afterwards by one of them, and dismasted. Not liking delay (for I am satisfied those two ships were the advance ones of the French squadron), and fancying we were close at their heels, they set fire to the vessel, and abandoned her in a hurry. If my explanation, gentlemen, be correct, I infer from it they are gone more to the northward, and more to the northward I will look for them.' Subsequent information proved that he was correct in every part of his interpretation."

Hoping to profit by the information, the fleet stood more to the north-ward. On the 12th August, the *Niobe* was spoken, three days from the Channel fleet, at which time no intelligence had been obtained of the enemy's arrival in any of the ports of the Bay of Biscay. On the 15th, they fell in with Admiral Cornwallis off Ushant, and in the evening Nelson received orders to proceed with the *Victory* and *Superb* to Portsmouth. A general feeling of regret, from Admiral Louis to the youngest boy, prevailed

throughout the fleet on parting with their gallant chief. "I look forward,"
said Hallowell, "with pleasure to your resuming the command of us, to
lead your old Mediterranean squadron to a victory which will give much
satisfaction to the country."

It was a noble and beautiful trait in Nelson's character, that he never
undervalued the actions of his brother officers. The gallantry and misfor-
tunes of Calder, which he learnt on arriving in the Channel, particularly
claimed his sympathy. Writing to Captain Fremantle, he said, "I was in
truth bewildered by the account of Sir Robert Calder's victory, and the joy
of the event, together with the hearing that the nation was not content,
which I am sorry for. Who can command all the success which our
country may wish for? We have fought together, and therefore well know
what it is. I have had the best-disposed fleet of friends, but who can say
what may be the event of a battle? And it most sincerely grieves me, that
in any of the papers it should be insinuated, 'Lord Nelson could have
done better.' I should have fought the enemy, so did my friend Calder.
Who can promise that he will be more successful than another? I only wish
to stand upon my own merits, and not by comparison, one way or the other,
with the conduct of a brother-officer." The *Victory* anchored at Spithead
on the 17th of August. "Just two years and three months," wrote Nelson,
"from my arrival in Portsmouth, in 1803."

The West India merchants, through their chairman, Sir R. Neave, Bart.,
were among the first, on the admiral's arrival in London, to express their
high sense of his prompt determination in quitting the Mediterranean, and
his sagacity in pursuing the combined fleet to the West Indies, and all
classes united in welcoming him after his long and arduous services.
Nelson's presence imparted vigour and firmness to the operations of
Government. Lord Barham, then First Lord of the Admiralty, on
receiving Nelson's journals, perused the whole narrative with attention, and
afterwards admitted he had not before sufficiently appreciated his extraordinary talents. This opinion was immediately communicated to the Cabinet,
with an assurance from Lord Barham, that an unbounded confidence ought
to be placed in Nelson; and that he was, above all others, the one to be
employed on the station he had so ably watched, and whose political
relations he so thoroughly understood.

Nelson's most anxious wish was to be once more in command of the fleet in which he was so universally beloved. The voice of the country was in strict unison with this desire. "In some occasional interviews with Lord Barham at the Admiralty, he now expressed his readiness to obey the voice of his country, and pointed out various means by which additional effect might be given to the service on which he was about to be employed. He visited also the other departments of Government, opened his mind without reserve or fear, and traced, with the decision and even authority of a statesman, the various plans that required immediate attention. He showed ministers the dangers to which they were particularly exposed in the Mediterranean, the errors which had too long been persisted in, and the events and changes that might be expected to take place in Europe, from the prevailing aspect of its political horizon. At many of these ministerial conferences, the late Admiral Sir Richard Keats attended his friend ; who frequently appealed to him, particularly in their last interview with Mr. Pitt, for the truth of what he asserted, and also for further information on those subjects, of which the liberal mind of Nelson confessed that Keats had a greater knowledge than himself." During one of Nelson's visits to the Admiralty previous to leaving England, the list of the navy was given him by Lord Barham, who desired him to choose his own officers. Nelson returned it, saying, "Choose yourself, my lord ; the same spirit actuates the whole profession ; you cannot choose wrong." Lord Barham then desired that the admiral would, without reserve, dictate to the private secretary the names of the ships he wished, in addition to his present squadron. It was owing to this unlimited confidence on the part of Lord Barham that the Mediterranean fleet received constant reinforcements, which, from not sailing in a body, arrived without information of them reaching the enemy.

Towards the end of August, Captain Blackwood arrived in the *Euryalus*, with the news of the blockade of the combined fleets in Cadiz. On his way to London with the despatches, he called at Merton about five o'clock in the morning. Nelson was already up and dressed. On seeing Blackwood, he exclaimed, "I am sure you bring me news of the French and Spanish fleets, and I think I shall yet have to beat them." Captain Blackwood briefly told him the news, and, after expressing hopes that he should be present on the occasion, left for the Admiralty. Nelson was not long in following, and everything was speedily arranged for his departure.

On the night of Friday, September 13th, having taken leave of his brother William, Lady Hamilton, and his friends who were at Merton, Nelson, with a mind much agitated, pursued his route to Portsmouth—" to serve " as he expressed himself in his diary, "his king and country." He appeared, from his conversations with the Duke of Clarence and with Lord Sidmouth, to anticipate a desperate battle, and to have a strong presentiment of never returning. On leaving Merton, he offered up the following sublime prayer to the God of battles :—" May the great God whom I adore enable me to fulfil the expectations of my country ; and if it be His good pleasure that I should return, my thanks will never cease being offered up to the throne of His mercy. If it be His good providence to cut short my days upon earth, I bow with the greatest submission, relying that He will protect those so dear to me whom I may leave behind. His will be done.—Amen."

" He arrived at the George Inn, Portsmouth, at six in the following morning, and having arranged everything with his accustomed quickness, went to that part of the beach to embark for the *Victory*, where the bathing machines are placed. The scene is described as having been singularly affecting. He was followed by numbers of his countrymen in tears, many of whom knelt down before him, and blessed the beloved hero of the British nation. The affectionate heart of Nelson could not but sympathise with the great interest that was taken in his welfare, and, turning round to Captain Hardy, he said :—' I had their huzzas before—I have their hearts now.' A fresh proof of the attachment of the common seamen to him had also appeared ; the crew of the *Superb*, Captain Keats, which ship, owing to her necessary repairs, was not ready for sea, were heard to express their desire that they might be turned over to some ship in the harbour which was ready, in order to go back with their admiral to the Mediterranean. Mr. Rose and Mr. Canning accompanied Lord Nelson to his ship, and dined on board whilst the *Victory* was preparing to sail. *

Writing to Mr. Davison, he said :—" Day by day, my dear friend, I am expecting the fleet to put to sea—every day, hour, and moment ; and you may rely that, if it is in the power of man to get at them, it shall be done ; and I am sure that all my brethren look to that day as the finish of our anxious cruise. The event no man can say exactly, but I must think, or render great injustice to those under me, that, let the battle be when it may, it will never have been surpassed. My shattered frame, if I survive that day, will require rest, and that is all I shall ask for. If I fall on such a glorious occasion, it shall be my pride to take care that my friends shall not blench for me. These things are in the hands of a wise and just Providence, and His will be done. I have got some trifle, thank God, to leave to those I hold most dear, and I have taken care not to neglect it. Do not think I am low-spirited on this account, or fancy anything is to happen to me; quite the contrary—my mind is calm, and I have only to think of destroying our inveterate foe." The *Victory* weighed on the 15th, at daybreak, accompanied by Captain Blackwood, in the *Euryalus*. The ships had to work down channel against strong winds. On the 17th, when off Plymouth, Nelson sent in the *Euryalus* to call out the *Ajax* and *Thunderer*.

After a stormy passage, the *Victory* arrived off Cadiz on the 29th of September, on which day Nelson completed his forty-seventh year. Since the 22nd of August, Collingwood had blockaded the enemy with eighteen sail of the line, when he was relieved by the arrival of the *Victory*. Nelson, desirous that there should be no saluting, which would inform the enemy of his arrival, or of that of a reinforcement, ordered the *Euryalus* to precede him, and request Collingwood to withhold the customary compliment. The British fleet now numbered twenty-seven sail of the line, which brought it nearly upon an equality with the fleets of Spain and France.

When Nelson joined he found the fleet too near the harbour of Cadiz, which was distant not more than fifteen miles: the in-shore squadron consisted of five sail of the line. He therefore determined to stand further off, and to cruise sixteen or eighteen leagues to the westward of Cadiz, near Cape St. Mary. His object in this move was in order to decoy the enemy out of port, while at the same time he guarded against the danger of being caught in a westerly gale, and being driven through the Straits.

During his career Nelson had surprisingly escaped from professional enemies—two only he was acquainted with; and the manner in which he requited ill services was beautifully shown in his conduct to one of the number then under his command. He had been the bearer of a message from Lord Barham to Sir Robert Calder, touching the recent action off

Ferrol. Nelson advised Calder to remain until after the action then about to ensue, but was unable to persuade him. Writing to Lord Barham, he said :—" I did not fail, immediately on my arrival, to deliver your message to Sir Robert Calder, and it will give your lordship pleasure to find, as it has me, that an inquiry is what the vice-admiral wishes, and that he had written to you to say so. Sir Robert thinks that he can clearly prove it was not in his power to bring the combined squadrons again to battle. Sir Robert felt so much, even at the idea of being removed from his own ship which he commanded, in the face of the fleet, that I much fear I shall incur the censure of the Board of Admiralty, for parting with a 90-gun ship before the force arrives which their lordships have judged necessary. But I trust that I shall be considered to have done right as a man, and to a brother-officer in affliction—my heart could not stand it."

Nelson's reception on rejoining the fleet gave him great delight. The officers who repaired on board to welcome his return greeted him with the utmost enthusiasm.

Nelson had reduced the in-shore squadron to the *Hydra* and *Euryalus* frigates, and outside of them, at a convenient distance for signalling, he stationed four sail of the line. On the 1st of October the *Euryalus* recon-noitred the port of Cadiz, and counted in the outer harbour eighteen French and sixteen Spanish ships of the line, apparently ready for sea. Between the 9th and 13th the *Royal Sovereign*, *Belleisle*, *Africa*, and *Agamemnon* joined the fleet; but five sail, under Rear-Admiral Louis, having been despatched to Gibraltar for provisions and water, the number was again brought down to twenty-seven sail. Since the 10th the enemy's fleet had moved towards the entrance of the harbour, and evinced a disposition to put to sea. From the 10th to the 17th the wind continued to blow fresh from the westward, which kept them in; but, on the 17th, at midnight, it shifted to the eastward. On Saturday, the 19th, at 7h. A.M., the combined fleet weighed, with a light breeze from the northward. Owing to the lightness of the wind, however, only twelve ships got out, and these lay becalmed until the afternoon, when a breeze sprang up from the westward, and this division of the enemy stood to the northward, closely watched by the *Euryalus* and *Sirius*, which immediately signalled the cheering news to the British fleet.

On this morning Nelson was more than usually anxious, and he came on deck under the full impression that the enemy's fleet had put to sea. No signal to that effect had then been made by the look-out frigates, but his lordship persisted in his belief that such a signal was flying. Both the signal-lieutenant, Pasco, and Captain Hardy went to the mast-head with their glasses to ascertain whether any such signal was out, but were unable to discover anything leading them to suppose that such was the case. About an hour afterwards a signal-gun announced that the enemy had put to sea.

At daylight, on the 20th, the remainder of the enemy's fleet put to sea with a breeze from the south-east ; but had scarcely cleared the harbour when the wind changed to south-west, attended with thick weather. At 2h. P.M. the wind shifted to west-north-west, and the weather cleared up. Napoleon was so much dissatisfied with Villeneuve's conduct in the action with Sir Robert Calder, that he appointed Vice-Admiral Rosily to succeed him, but that admiral not having arrived, Villeneuve remained in command, having under him the Spanish Vice-Admiral d'Alava and Rear-Admiral Dumanoir. The second part of the fleet, or reserve, was divided into two squadrons of six ships each ; the first under the Spanish Admiral Gravina, and the second commanded by Rear-Admiral Magon.

A little before daybreak, on Monday the 21st, finding that the British were to windward, the French admiral directed the three columns of the line of battle, in which the fleet was formed, to draw, without regard to priority of rank among the captains, into a close line of battle on the starboard tack, and to steer south-west. At daylight the two fleets were about twelve miles apart, the centre of the combined fleet bearing about east-by-south from the centre of the British, the wind being light from west-north-west, accompanied by a long ground swell. At 6h. A.M. the enemy was distinctly seen from the decks of the British ships, the *Victory* being at this time distant from Cape Trafalgar about seven leagues. At 6h. 40m. Lord Nelson made the signals to form the order of sailing in two columns and prepare for battle, and, in a few minutes afterwards, to bear up. At 8h. 30m. Villeneuve made the signal for his fleet to wear and form a line in close order on the larboard tack ; but, owing to the light air of wind and the great swell, it was not until 10h. that this movement was completed, and even then the line, if such it could be called, was very irregularly formed—so much so, that it was nearly in the shape of a crescent, and, instead of the ships being in line ahead, some were at a distance to leeward, and others to windward, of their proper stations. For the most part the ships were two, and, in some cases, three abreast, and they were generally under topsails and topgallant-sails, with maintopsails on their masts.

"Soon after daylight," says Dr. Beatty, "Lord Nelson came upon deck; he was dressed as usual in his admiral's frock-coat, bearing on the left breast four stars of different orders, which he always wore with his common apparel. He did not wear his sword in the battle of Trafalgar,—it had been taken from the place where it hung up in his cabin, and was laid ready on his table; but it is supposed he forgot to call for it. This was the only action in which he ever appeared without a sword. He displayed excellent spirits, and expressed his pleasure at the prospect of giving a fatal blow to the naval power of France and Spain, and spoke with a confidence of obtaining a signal victory, notwithstanding the inferiority of the British fleet, declaring to Captain Hardy that ' he would not be contented with capturing less than twenty sail of the line.' He afterwards pleasantly observed, ' that the 21st of October was the happiest day in the year among his family,' but did not assign the reason of this. His lordship had previously entertained a strong presentiment that this would prove the auspicious day; and had several times said to Captain Hardy and Doctor Scott (chaplain of the ship and foreign secretary to the commander-in-chief, whose intimate friendship he enjoyed), ' The 21st of October will be our day.'"

The wind was so light, that although the British ships had studding-sails on both sides, they did not go more than two knots an hour, and scarcely that; and while the fleet was thus slowly nearing the enemy, Nelson visited the different decks of the *Victory*, cautioning the men not to fire without being sure of their object. At about eleven o'clock, Lieutenant Pasco, having to make a report to Lord Nelson, and intending at the same time to represent to his lordship that he considered himself unfortunate on such an occasion—being the senior lieutenant—to be doing duty as signal officer, proceeded to the admiral's cabin. "On entering," said he, "I discovered his lordship on his knees writing. He was then penning that beautiful prayer. I waited until he rose, and communicated what I had to report, but could not at such a moment disturb his mind with any grievances of my own." The following is the prayer referred to :—" May the Great God, whom I worship, grant to my country, and for the benefit of Europe in general, a great and glorious victory ; and may no misconduct in any one tarnish it ; and may humanity after victory be the predominant feature in the British fleet ! For myself individually, I commit my life to Him that made me ; and may His blessing alight on my endeavours for serving my country faithfully ! To Him I resign myself and the great cause which is entrusted me to defend. Amen, amen, amen."

Thinking that the *Victory*, as the flag-ship and leader of the column, would draw the principal attention of the enemy's fire, it was proposed to Nelson, by Captain Blackwood, that the *Téméraire* should go ahead of her ; and to this proposal Lord Nelson replied, "Oh, yes, let her go ahead ! " but at the same time had no intention of allowing her, nor would he permit an inch of canvas to be taken in. The *Victory* continued, therefore, to lead the column, closely hugged by the *Téméraire*. Apprehensive that the enemy might run for Cadiz, then at no great distance under their lee, Nelson telegraphed to Collingwood, " I intend to pass through the van of the enemy's line, to prevent him from getting into Cadiz." At 11 h. 40 m. A.M., Lord Nelson ordered his last and never-to-be-forgotten telegraphic signal to be made, " ENGLAND EXPECTS THAT EVERY MAN WILL DO HIS DUTY ; " and the purport of this signal having been communicated to the men at their quarters, it was greeted with three hearty cheers, and excited the most lively enthusiasm among officers and men. In reference to this signal, Rear-Admiral John Pasco, who was signal-lieutenant of the *Victory* at the time, has stated that Lord Nelson first gave directions to make the signal, " England *confides*," &c., but that the word " confides " not being in the vocabulary, Lieutenant Pasco suggested the word " expects," to which his lordship immediately assented.

The *Fougueux*, the ship next astern to the *Santa Ana*, about ten minutes before noon, fired a shot to try the range of her guns, upon which the *Victory* and all the British ships hoisted their colours. Both divisions of the fleet wore the St. George's ensign, the better to distinguish the colours from those of the enemy, also a union jack on the foretop-mast-stay and many on the maintop-mast-stay. Shortly afterwards the combined fleets hoisted their colours ; and the *Santa Ana*, with several ships ahead and astern, commenced a heavy fire upon the *Royal Sovereign*, then bearing from the *Victory* south-east two miles, and from the *Belleisle* east-by-north, distant about a quarter of a mile. At ten minutes past noon, the *Royal Sovereign* commenced the action by passing close under the stern of the *Santa Ana*, discharging every gun of her larboard broadside as it came to bear, then luffing round she took up her station on the starboard bow of her opponent. In breaking through the line the *Royal Sovereign* fired her starboard broadside into the *Fougueux*.

The feelings of the two noble admirals almost at the same moment found utterance : Collingwood, as his ship was thus gallantly commencing the fight, observed to Captain Rotheram, "What would Nelson give to be here?" and at the same instant Nelson, observing his friend in his enviable position, exclaimed, "See how nobly Collingwood carries his ship into action."

The *Royal Sovereign* was followed by the *Belleisie, Mars*, and other ships of the lee line, and all of which were closely engaged, before the *Victory* could get into action.

The weather column, led by the *Victory*, steered a more northerly course than the lee line, Nelson being anxious, as before observed, to prevent the enemy's escape into Cadiz. Nelson's object was now to single out the flag ship of Admiral Villeneuve ; but although all the glasses on board the ship were in requisition, the flag could not be discovered. In this dilemma, Nelson determined to steer for his old aquaintance the *Santisima Trinidad*, rightly conjecturing that he should thus hit upon Villeneuve also.

As the *Victory* rolled down at a sluggish pace towards the enemy, Nelson's anxiety was so great, that it caused him to disregard the suggestions of caution. He would not permit the hammocks to be stowed higher than usual, because they would have obscured his view of the enemy's ships. And yet his mind was intent at the same time to guard against any injury to his ship. The hammocks were, as usual, covered with black painted cloths ; but knowing the danger to be apprehended from fire in the close action to which the ship was about to be subjected, he gave directions for the white canvas cloths to be brought up from below, and spread over all. These being thoroughly saturated with water, doubtless afforded much protection during the action.

At about twenty minutes past noon, the *Bucentaure* fired a shot at the *Victory*. The shot fell short, but in two or three minutes, a second shot pitched close alongside ; a third and fourth followed in quick succession, one passing over the ship, and another making a hole in the maintop-gallant sail, thus giving a visible proof that the ship was within range. A minute's awful pause ensued, and then, as if by the signal, seven or eight ships opened a fire upon the *Victory* of the most destructive and trying kind. Mr. Scott, the admiral's secretary, while conversing with Captain Hardy, was shot dead.' Judging from the course pursued by the lee division that it was the British admiral's intention to pass through the line also, the enemy closed towards that point to which the *Victory* was advancing. The *Santa Ana*, however, remaining stationary, engaged by the *Sovereign*, and the ships near her having full employment from the immediate followers of Collingwood, the enemy's fleet was divided nearly in the centre—leaving fourteen ships in the van, and nineteen in the rear divisions, with a space of nearly a mile between them.

The *Victory* had arrived within 500 or 600 yards of the enemy, when her mizen top-mast was shot away, and also her wheel, so that she was obliged to be steered by the relieving tackles below. A shot about this time killed eight marines on the poop, after which Captain Adair, by Lord Nelson's request, ordered his men to lie down. Shortly afterwards, a splinter from the fore-brace bits passed between Nelson and Hardy, and a part of it tore away the buckle from the shoe of the latter. Both looked earnestly and anxiously, each supposing the other to have been injured. Nelson smiled, and said, "'This is too warm work to last long, Hardy." Captain Hardy remarked the impossibility of getting through the cluster of ships a-head without running foul of one of them, to which his lordship quickly replied, " I cannot help it ; it does not signify which we run on board of ; go on board which you please : take your choice."

By this time the *Victory* (whose sails were hanging in tatters) had lost full fifty men killed and wounded ; but it was now her turn to begin. Having at length determined to pass under the stern of the *Bucentaure* as the only mode of breaking the line, the *Victory's* helm, at about 1h. P.M., was put hard a-port, but there was scarcely space enough to enable her to go clear. The *Victory*, therefore, passed so close to the larboard side of the

Bucentaure that, as she poured her well directed and tremendous broadside into that ship, the effect of it was so great that the French ship was observed to heel two or three streaks on receiving it. The *Victory* then hauled round as close under the stern of the French ship as was practicable, in the hope of bringing her to action to leeward ; but this was prevented by the advance of the *Redoutable*, a collision with which ship quickly took place.

The best bower anchor of the *Victory*, and the spare anchor of the *Redoutable*, were broken by the blow, and the concussion drove the latter ship round off, nearly before the wind. This happened at about 1h. 10m. P.M. The ships would, however, in all probability, have separated, had not their yard-arms been foul, which kept them together. The larboard broadside of the *Victory* was, therefore, constantly employed upon the *Bucentaure* and *Santisima*, but principally upon the latter, and her starboard gun found full employment with the *Redoutable*, her immediate opponent.

Nelson continued pacing the quarter-deck with Hardy, their walk being bounded abaft by the wheel, and forward by the companion ladder, a distance of about twenty-five feet only. At 1h. 25m. his lordship was about to turn to walk aft, when he received the fatal bullet. Hardy, turning, observed his admiral in the act of falling ; and before he could prevent it his lordship was on his knees, with his left hand just touching the deck, very near to the same spot whereon his secretary, Mr. Scott, had fallen. On Captain Hardy's expressing a hope that his lordship was not severely wounded, Nelson said, " They have done for me at last, Hardy." " I hope not," replied the captain. " Yes," continued his lordship ; " my backbone is shot through." A musket-ball had entered the left shoulder, through the strap of the epaulette, and, descending, had lodged in the spine. Sergeant Secker, of the marines, and two seamen, conveyed the wounded hero to the cockpit.

The direction taken by the bullet proves that it must have been fired from aloft, and that it came from the mizen-top of the *Redoutable ;* but there is scarcely sufficient reason for believing that it was aimed in particular at Nelson. It was most probably a chance shot, but, notwithstanding this, the direction from which it came led to the destruction of every man in the mizen-top of the *Redoutable.* Captain Adair immediately snatched up a musket, and with a midshipman, Mr. John Pollard, and many others, continued to fire at the men in the mizen-top of the *Redoutable*, until one by one they were observed to fall.

The loss had been so severe on the quarter-deck and poop of the *Victory*, that Captain Hardy, Captain Adair, of the marines, and two or three officers, were nearly all who remained. Observing the deserted appearance of the deck, the captain of the *Redoutable* ordered an attempt to be made to board ; but the remaining marines, assisted by a few small-arm men, kept up so continual and animated a fire, that the men assembled in the main-rigging with this intention were shot down as fast as they appeared. In repelling this attack, the gallant Adair was killed, and Lieutenant Ram mortally, and Mr. George A. Westphal, midshipman, severely wounded ; many seamen and marines also fell.

As Nelson was being conveyed below, Dr. Beatty states that he caused his face and stars to be covered by his handkerchief, in order that he might pass unnoticed by the crew. On reaching the cockpit, the dying hero was laid upon a midshipman's mattress, and stripped of his clothes, when the surgeon proceeded to probe the wound, which he soon ascertained to be mortal, an opinion which Nelson had from the first entertained. The sufferings of his lordship, from pain and thirst, were very great. In about an hour and ten minutes after Nelson had been carried below, Hardy, availing himself of a moment's respite from his duties, visited his dying admiral. "They shook hands," says Dr. Beatty, "very affectionately, and Nelson said, 'Well, Hardy, how goes the battle? How goes the day with us?' 'Very well, my lord,' replied Hardy. 'We have got twelve or fourteen of the enemy's ships in our possession ; but five of their van have tacked and show an intention of bearing down upon the *Victory*; I have, therefore, called two or three of our fresh ships round us, and have no doubt of giving them a drubbing.' 'I hope,' said his lordship, 'none of *our* ships have struck, Hardy.' 'No, my lord,' replied Hardy, 'there is no fear of that.' Lord Nelson then said, 'I am a dead man, Hardy, I am going fast ; it will be all over with me soon.'" Hardy In a minute or two returned to the deck, and the *Victory* soon afterwards opened her fire upon Dumanoir's squadron, passing to windward, as before described. The concussion of the firing caused great distress to his lordship ; and, apostro- phizing his ship, he exclaimed, "Oh, *Victory, Victory*, how you distract my poor brain!" The *Orion* and other ships having neared the *Victory*, Dumanoir and his squadron hauled their wind to the southward, offering no further molestation.

In about fifty minutes after Hardy had returned to the deck, he a second time descended to the cockpit, and again shook hands with Lord Nelson, at the same moment congratulating him on the brilliant victory the British fleet had achieved ; and, although unable to ascertain the exact number of the enemy's ships that had struck, he was certain that fourteen or fifteen had surrendered. His lordship answered, " That is well, but I bargained for twenty ;" and then emphatically exclaimed, "Anchor, Hardy, anchor !" "I suppose, my lord," continued Captain Hardy, "that Admiral Colling-wood will now take upon himself the direction of affairs?" " Not while I live, I hope, Hardy," cried the dying hero ; and endeavouring ineffectually to raise himself from the bed, exclaimed, " No! do *you* anchor, Hardy !" Captain Hardy then said, "Shall *we* make the signal, Sir?" " Yes," answered his lordship, "for if I live, I'll anchor." Captain Hardy, after remaining about three minutes with his dying chief, went on deck.

" Lord Nelson," says Dr. Beatty, " now desired Chevalier, his steward, to turn him upon his right side ; which, being effected, his lordship said, ' I wish I had not left the deck, for I shall soon be gone.' He afterwards became very low, his breathing was oppressed, and his voice faint. He said to Dr. Scott, ' I have *not* been a *great* sinner:' and after a short pause, ' *Remember* that I leave Lady Hamilton and my daughter Horatia as a legacy to my country ; and,' added he, ' never forget Horatia.' His thirst now increased, and he called, ' Drink, drink—fan, fan—rub, rub :' addressing himself in the last case to Dr. Scott, who had been rubbing his lordship's breast with his hand, from which he felt some relief. These words he spoke in a very rapid manner, which rendered his articulation difficult : but he every now and then, with evident increase of pain, made a greater effort with his vocal powers, and pronounced distinctly these last words, ' Thank God, I have done my duty,' and this great sentiment he continued to repeat as long as he was able to give it utterance. He breathed his last at thirty minutes past four o'clock."

The moment the event was announced to Captain Hardy, he directed Lieutenant A. Hills to proceed to the *Royal Sovereign*, and acquaint

Admiral Collingwood that Nelson was mortally wounded, not wishing to hurt the feelings of a friend, by stating that he was dead. Captain Black-wood arrived on board the *Victory* soon afterwards, and Captain Hardy accompanied him, in the boat of the *Euryalus*, to the *Royal Sovereign*, to acquaint the vice-admiral with what had really happened, as well as to deliver Nelson's dying commands, that the fleet should be brought to anchor as soon as it was practicable. Vice-Admiral Collingwood differed in this respect with his distinguished friend, and on receiving the message, replied, "Anchor the fleet ! Why, it is the last thing I should have thought of."

At the conclusion of the action, the land about Cape Trafalgar was in sight, bearing south-east-by-east, distant about eight miles, after which cape the battle was named.

The names of the officers officially returned killed and wounded, were:— *Victory*, killed: Vice-Admiral Lord Nelson; John Scott, secretary; Capt. (Marines) Charles W. Adair; Lieut. W. Ram; Mids. Robert Smith and Alexander Palmer; Captain's Clerk Thomas Whipple. Wounded: Lieuts. John Pasco and George M. Bligh; Lieuts. (Marines) Lewis B. Reeves and James G. Peake; Mids. Wm. Rivers, Geo. A. Westphal, and Richard Bulkeley.—*Téméraire*, killed: Captain (Marines) Simeon Busigny ; Lieut. do.) John Kingston; Carpenter Lewis Oades; Mid. Wm. Pitts. Wounded: Lieut. Jas. Mould; Lieut. (Marines) Sam. J. Payne; Boatsw. J. Brooks; Mate F. S. Price; Midshipman J. Eastman.—*Neptune*, wounded: Cap-tain's clerk. —*Leviathan*, wounded: J. W. Watson, mid. —*Britannia*, killed: Lieut. Fras. Roskruge. Wounded: Steph. Trounce, master; William Grant, midshipman.—*Conqueror*, killed: Lieuts. Robt. Lloyd and W. St. George. Wounded: Lieut. (Marines) Thos. Wearing; Lieut. (Russian Navy) Philip Mendel.—*Africa*, wounded: Lieut. Matthew Hay; Capt. (Marines) Jas. Fynmore; Mates Henry West and Ab. Turner; Mids. Fred. White, P. J. Elmhurst, and J. P. Bailey.—*Orion*, wounded: Chas. Tause and T. P. Cable, midshipmen.—*Minotaur*, wounded: Jas. Robinson, boat-swain; J. S. Smith, midshipman.—*Spartiate*, wounded: John Clarke, boatswain; Mids. Edward Bellairs and Edw. Knapman.—*Royal Sovereign*, killed: Lieut, Brice Gilliland ; Master Wm. Chalmers; Lieut. (Marines) Robert Green; Mids. John Aikenhead and Thomas Braund. Wounded: Lieuts. John Clavell and James Bachford ; Lieut. (Marines) Jas. Le Vesconte ;

Mate W. Watson; Mids. G. Kennicott, Grenville Thompson, J. Farrant, and John Campbell; Boatswain Isaac Wilkinson.—*Belleisle*, killed: Lieuts. Ebenr. Gale and John Woodin; Mid. Geo. Nind. Wounded: Lieut. Wm. Ferrie; Lieut. (Marines) John Owen; Boatswain Andrew Gibson; Mates W. H. Pearson, W. Cutfield; Mids. Sam. Jago and J. T. Hodge.—*Mars*, killed: Captain Duff; Mids. Ed. Corbyn and Hen. Morgan. Wounded: Lieuts. Ed. Wm. Garrett and Jas. Black; Master Thomas Cook; Capt. (Marines) T. Norman; Mids. J. Young, Geo. Guiren, W. J. Cook, J. Jenkins, and Alfred Luckraft. — *Tonnant*, killed: Mid. Wm. Brown. Wounded: Capt. Tyler; Lieut. Fred. Hoffman; Boatswain Richard Little · Mate H. Ready; Captain's Clerk W. Allen.—*Bellerophon*, killed: Capt. Cooke; Master Edward Overton; Mid. John Simmons. Wounded: Capt. (Marines) John Wemyss; Boatswain Th. Robinson; Mate E. Hartley; Mids. W. N. Jewell, Jas. Stone, Thos. Bant, and George Pearson.—*Colossus*, killed: Thomas Scriven, master. Wounded: Captain Morris; Lieuts. George Bully and Wm. Forster; Lieut. (Marines) J. Benson; Boatswain Wm. Adamson; Mate Henry Millbanke; Mids. W. A. Herringham, F. Thistlewayte, T. G. Reece, H. Snellgrove, R. M'Lean, George Wharrie, Tim. Renou, and George Denton.—*Achille*, killed: Mid. J. F. Mugg. Wounded: Lieuts. Parkins Prynn and Josias Bray; Capt. (Marines) Palms Westropp and Lieut. Wm. Liddon; Mate G. Pegge; Mids. W. H. Staines, W. J. Snow, and W. Smith Warren.—*Dreadnought*, wounded: Lieut. J. L. Loyd; Mids. Andrew M'Cullock and James Sabben. — *Revenge*, killed: Thos. Grier and Edward F. Brooks, midshipmen. Wounded: Capt. Moorsom; Lieut. John Berry; Master Luke Brokenshaw; Capt. (Marines) Peter Lely.—*Swiftsure*, wounded: Alex. Benjamin Handcock, midshipman. *Defiance*, killed: Lieut. Thomas Simmons; Boatswain W. Forster; Mid. James Williamson. Wounded: Captain Durham; Mates James Spratt and Robert Browne; Midshipmen J. Hodge and Ed. And. Chapman.—*Thunderer*, wounded: Mate John Snell; Mid. Alex. Galloway.

A question having some time since arisen as to whether Lord Nelson went into action with one or more stars on his breast, Sir George Westphal, who was a midshipman of the *Victory* in the action, was appealed to, and the following is his statement :—" From the period of his flag being hoisted at Spithead, at the commencement of hostilities with France in 1803, to the hour of his death, *I have no recollection of ever seeing him wear a full-dress uniform coat on board the Victory*, or elsewhere ; and I am most positive that the coat which his lordship wore on the day the battle was fought was an *old undress uniform*, the skirts being lined with white shalloon or linen, The *four* orders that he *invariably* wore were embroidered on the breast of every coat I had ever seen him wear from his first hoisting his flag. They were placed thus *** on the left breast of his coat—the order of the Bath being uppermost. I feel persuaded that you cannot have better authority than my own for the truth of this disputed question, because when I was carried down wounded, I was placed by the side of his lordship, and his coat was rolled up, and put as the substitute for a pillow under my head, which was then bleeding very much from the wound I had received ; and when the battle was over, and an attempt made to remove the coat, several of the bullions of the epaulette were found to be so firmly glued into my hair by the coagulated blood from my wound, that the bullions, four or five of them, were cut off, and left in my hair, one of which I have still in my possession."

There not being sufficient lead in the ship of which to make a coffin, the body of Nelson was placed in a leaguer filled with brandy. On the arrival of the *Victory* at Gibraltar, on the 28th of October, spirits of wine was substituted for the brandy, and in this the mortal remains were brought to England. The badly wounded were landed at Gibraltar on the 29th, and on the 3rd November, having re-embarked several of the wounded, the *Victory* sailed with her mournful freight, and after a tedious passage, arrived at Spithead on the 5th of December. Here Captain Hardy eventually received orders to convey his freight to the Nore. On the 11th the *Victory* sailed, but strong easterly winds prevailing, she did not reach Sheerness until the 22nd.

After leaving Spithead, Dr. Beatty represented to Captain Hardy the necessity for examining the body of his lordship to ascertain if decomposition had taken place, it having been reported that the body was not only to lie in state at Greenwich Hospital, but that the features were to be exposed to the public gaze. Captain Hardy having assented, the cask was opened and the body taken therefrom. During this examination the course and site of the ball were ascertained. It had passed through the spine, and had lodged in the muscles of the back towards the right side, and a little below the shoulder blade. A very considerable portion of the gold lace, pad, and lining of the epaulette, with a piece of the coat, was found attached to the ball—the lace of the epaulette was as firmly so as if it had been inserted in the metal while in a state of fusion. The remains, after undergoing examination, were wrapped in cotton vestments, and rolled from head to foot with bandages of the same material. The body was then put into a leaden coffin, which was filled with brandy, holding in solution camphor and myrrh, and placed in the admiral's cabin. This was subsequently deposited in the coffin made from the mainmast of *L'Orient* and the whole enclosed in a wooden shell. On the 22nd the commissioners' yacht belonging to Chatham took the corpse on board, and proceeded with it to Greenwich Hospital.

Dr. Beatty gives the following interesting particulars of the hero :—"His lordship had on several occasions told Captain Hardy that if he should fall in battle in a foreign climate, he wished his body to be conveyed to England ; and that if his country should think proper to inter him at the public expense, he wished to be buried in St. Paul's, as well as that his monument should be erected there. He explained his reasons for preferring St. Paul's to Westminster Abbey, which were rather curious. He said that he remembered hearing it stated as an old tradition, when he was a boy, that Westminster Abbey was built on a spot where once existed a deep morass ; and he thought it likely that the lapse of time would reduce the ground on which it now stands to its primitive state of a swamp, without leaving a trace of the abbey. He said that his observations confirmed the probability of this event. He repeated to Captain Hardy several times during the last two years of his life, 'Should I be killed, Hardy, and my country not bury me, you know what to do with me,' meaning that his body was in that case to be laid by the side of his father in his native village of Burnham Thorpe."

The Doctor adds :—"An opinion has been very generally entertained, that Lord Nelson's state of health and supposed infirmities, arising from his former wounds and hard services, precluded the probability of his long surviving the battle of Trafalgar, had he fortunately escaped the enemy's shot ; but the writer of this can assert that his lordship's health was uniformly good, with the exception of some slight attacks of indisposition, arising from accidental causes, and which never continued above two or three days, nor confined him in any degree with respect to either exercise or regimen. During the last twelve months of his life he complained only three times in this way. It is true that his lordship, about the meridian of life, had been subject to fits of the gout, which disease, however, as well as his constitutional tendency to it, he totally overcame by abstaining, for the space of nearly two years, from animal food, and wine, and all other fermented drink ; confining his diet to vegetables, and commonly milk and water. And it is also a fact, that early in life, when he first went to sea, he left off the use of salt, which he then believed to be the sole cause of scurvy, and never took it afterwards with his food.

" He used a great deal of exercise, generally walking on deck six or seven hours in the day. He always rose early, for the most part shortly after daybreak. He breakfasted in summer about six, and at seven in the winter ; and if not occupied in reading or writing despatches, or examining into the details of the fleet, he walked the quarter-deck the greater part of the forenoon, going down to his cabin occasionally to commit to paper such incidents or reflections as occurred to him during that time, and as might be hereafter useful to his country. He dined generally about half-past two o'clock. At his table there were seldom less than eight or nine persons, consisting of the different officers of the ship ; and when the weather and the service permitted, he very often had several of the admirals and captains in the fleet to dine with him. At dinner he was alike affable and attentive to every one. He ate very sparingly himself, the liver and wing of a fowl and a small plate of macaroni in general composing his meal, during which he occasionally took a glass of champagne. He never exceeded four glasses of wine after dinner, and seldom drank three ; and even those were diluted with either common or Bristol water.

" Few men subject to the vicissitudes of a naval life equalled his lordship in an habitual systematic mode of living. He possessed such a wonderful activity of mind, as even prevented him from taking ordinary repose, seldom enjoying two hours of uninterrupted sleep ; and on several occasions he did not quit the deck during the whole night. At these times he took no pains to protect himself from the effects of wet, or night air, wearing only a thin great coat ; and he has frequently, after having his clothes wet through with

rain, refused to have them changed, saying that the leather waistcoat which
he wore over his flannel one would secure him from complaint. He seldom
wore boots, and was consequently very liable to have his feet wet. When
this occurred, he has often been known to go down to his cabin, throw off
his shoes, and walk on the carpet in his stockings for the purpose of drying
the feet of them. He chose this uncomfortable expedient rather than give
his servants the trouble of assisting him to put on fresh stockings.

" From these circumstances it may be inferred, that though Lord Nelson's
constitution was not of that kind which is generally denominated strong,
yet it was not very susceptible of complaint from the common occasional
causes of disease necessarily attending a naval life. The only bodily pain
which he felt in consequence of his many wounds was a slight rheumatic
affection of the stump of his amputated arm on any sudden variation in the
state of the weather. His lordship had lost his right eye by a contusion
which he received at the siege of Calvi. The vision of the other was likewise considerably impaired : he always, therefore, wore a green shade over
his forehead to defend this eye from the effects of a strong light ; but as he
was in the habit of looking much through a glass, there is little doubt that
had he lived a few years longer, and continued at sea, he would have lost
his sight totally."

From the *post mortem* examination, the surgeon expressed an opinion that,
from the healthy appearance of the vital parts, there was every reason to
believe that his lordship might have lived to a great age. Southey's conclusion is not less true than sublime. " He cannot be said to have fallen
prematurely, whose work was done, nor ought he to be lamented who died
so full of honours, and at the height of human fame. The most triumphant
death is that of the martyr; the most awful that of the martyred patriot;
the most splendid that of the hero in the hour of victory; and if the chariot
and the horses of fire had been vouchsafed for Nelson's translation, he
could scarcely have departed in a brighter blaze of glory. He has left us
not indeed his mantle of inspiration ; but a name and an example which are
at this hour inspiring thousands of the youth of England—a name which is
our pride, and an example which will continue to be our shield and our
strength."

CONCLUSION.

—◆—

OUR narrative quitted the mortal remains of the great Nelson on the 22nd of December, 1805, when the coffin containing his remains was placed on board the Chatham yacht at the Nore. The vessel immediately proceeded up the river Thames, the coffin being simply covered with an ensign. All the ships in the river lowered their colours to the yacht as she passed up; and at Tilbury and Gravesend the forts fired minute-guns, the bells tolled, and afterwards rang a muffled peal. In the evening of the 23rd the body was received by Admiral Lord Hood, Governor of Greenwich Hospital, with the greatest privacy, at Greenwich, and deposited in a private apartment, where it remained until the requisite arrangements could be made for its lying in state in the Painted Hall.

The lying in state occupied three days, Sunday, Monday, and Tuesday, and on each day the Hall was crowded to suffocation. On Wednesday, the 8th of January, at ten o'clock, the heralds and naval officers, appointed to assist in the ceremony by water, assembled at the house of the Governor of Greenwich Hospital; and at half-past twelve the procession, the rear of which extended nearly to Woolwich, began to move. The body was placed on board the State barge. Every conceivable mark of respect was paid as the procession advanced, the Tower guns and the gun-boats in the procession firing minute-guns. The wind was strong and adverse, and the barge did not arrive at Whitehall Stairs till half-past three o'clock. Here the body was landed, and afterwards deposited at the Admiralty, where a large room was appropriately fitted up for its reception.

On the following day, being Thursday the 9th, at twelve o'clock, the grand procession towards St. Paul's began to move. The ceremony, though not at all partaking of the gorgeous character of that with which our great military hero was lately conveyed to the same resting-place, was affectingly sublime. Soldiers as well as sailors mingled their heartfelt regrets over the hero's tomb. All were aware that in Nelson the country had sustained a loss of the utmost importance, which might never be supplied. The universal feeling was one of deep sorrow, which the remembrance of the brilliant victory he had been so instrumental in gaining could scarcely lessen, —certainly not efface.

From the dome of the Cathedral depended foreign flags, trophies of the hero's victories, their tattered state quietly telling the story of the conquests they denoted. The whole formed the most impressive and splendid solemnity that had ever been witnessed.

At thirty-three minutes past five, the coffin descended by unseen machinery to its last resting-place. Anthems, composed for the occasion, were sung with overwhelming effect ; and that which concluded the mournful ceremony ended with "His body is buried in peace," the chorus being, "BUT HIS NAME LIVETH EVERMORE !"

An earldom was created in the person of his brother, and the title descends with an estate granted in parliament to the issue of his sisters.

THE END.